For Terry, my Halloween husband—T. W.

For my daughter Gracie, who gave me the last
rung on the ladder to reaching my dreams—B.D.

Copyright © 2003 by Tracey West. Illustrations © 2003 by Brian W.
Dow. All rights reserved. Published by Grosset & Dunlap, a division of
Penguin Young Readers Group, 345 Hudson Street, New York, NY
10014. GROSSET & DUNLAP is a trademark of Penguin Group (USA)
Inc. Published simultaneously in Canada. Printed in the U.S.A.

Library of Congress Cataloging-in-Publication Data is available.

ISBN 0-448-43224-2   A B C D E F G H I J

S.CREAM SHOP

Abracadanger

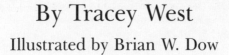

By Tracey West

Illustrated by Brian W. Dow

Grosset & Dunlap • New York

Ben Michaels adjusted the heavy pouch of newspapers over his shoulder and stared at the high hill ahead of him. He sighed. Old Man Martin had it in for him for sure. He had more hills on his route than any other carrier for the *Bleaktown News*.

At least it's the last block today, Ben thought as he trudged ahead. It was also payday. That thought made Ben's feet move a little faster.

With the five bucks he made today, he'd have saved up thirty dollars so far. That was half the money he needed to send away for the Official Junior Professional Magician's Kit.

His friend Lori thought he was crazy.

"You should save your money for a bicycle," she had said. "That would make your paper route a lot easier."

"But the whole reason I got the paper route was so I could buy a magic kit," Ben pointed out.

Lori shook her head. "Is magic all you think about?"

Ben didn't have to think twice. "Of course!" he replied.

Ben had been interested in magic ever since he

was seven, when he had seen a magician on TV pulling a rabbit out of a hat. He had spent the last five years reading every book in the Bleaktown library on magic tricks. Every penny he had went toward buying tricks at the toy store: the little plastic box that made a quarter appear and reappear, a specially marked deck of cards, three plastic rings that he could magically pull apart.

But Ben was tired of doing ordinary magic tricks. Sure, little kids were amazed when he pulled a scarf out of thin air, but that was amateur stuff. Ben wanted to be a really great magician someday—as great as the legendary Harry Houdini, his idol.

That's where the Official Junior Professional Magic Kit came in. The ad in *Junior Magician* magazine said that it contained tricks performed by the world's greatest magicians. Ben couldn't wait to get it. It would only take six more weeks to earn another thirty dollars, and then the kit would be his.

Ben reached the top of the hill and tossed out the last newspaper in his pouch. Finally. He turned the corner and headed downtown to the newspaper office.

The clock tower at Bleaktown Town Hall chimed four times. But the gray, gloomy sky made the day seem later than it was. Sunny afternoons did not happen often in Bleaktown.

That's probably why they call it Bleaktown, Ben realized for the first time. *This place sure is bleak.* Every house in Bleaktown was either gray, dingy white, or dusty brown. The downtown stores all had grimy windows and sold boring things like eyeglasses and insurance.

But there was nothing boring or bleak about magic tricks. To Ben, the most exciting thing in the world was the look on someone's face when he got a trick right.

It's too bad magic's not real, Ben thought as he climbed the steps to the *Bleaktown News* office. *Then I could make another thirty dollars appear out of thin air and quit this dumb paper route.*

Ben picked up his five dollars from Old Man Martin. Then he turned off of Main Street onto Wary Lane, a shortcut he sometimes took. The stores on Wary Lane were even more boring than the ones on Main Street. There was Just Lampshades. Mel's Medical Supply. Sebastian Cream's Curiosity Shop . . .

"What?" Ben stopped short. He'd never seen Sebastian Cream's Curiosity Shop before. In fact he didn't remember there even *being* a store next to Mel's. He walked up to the window and looked inside.

All kinds of unusual items cluttered the window

display. Ben saw a golden dragon statue with glittering red eyes. There were stacks of books, written in different languages, piled high. Old-fashioned windup toys crawled and hopped along the top of a display table.

And then Ben saw it: An old, beat-up-looking box, with the words DR. PRESTO'S MAGIC KIT.

Ben gasped. Every book about magicians he had ever read had a chapter about Dr. Presto. He was a world-famous magician who had performed some of the most incredible illusions in the business. Then in 1922 he had mysteriously vanished, never to be heard from again.

Could this really be Dr. Presto's kit? The box's front also had a small picture of a bearded man with silk wrapped around his head. It looked like Dr. Presto, all right.

Ben opened the door and stepped inside the shop.

"May I help you?"

It took Ben a second to realize that the voice was coming from behind a counter in the back of the room. A man sat on a stool behind the counter, writing in a book with a feather quill pen. He looked rather short and round. A ring of white hair circled his otherwise bald head. Two bright green eyes peered at Ben through a pair of wire-rimmed glasses.

"Sebastian Cream, at your service," the man said, handing Ben a business card:

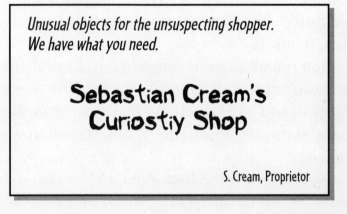

Unusual objects for the unsuspecting shopper.
We have what you need.

Sebastian Cream's Curiostiy Shop

S. Cream, Proprietor

"May I help you?" Sebastian Cream asked again.

"Uh, yeah," Ben said. "That magic kit in the window. Did that really belong to Dr. Presto?"

Mr. Cream smiled. "Ah, I see you are a fan of the art of illusion," he said. "Yes, that kit did indeed belong to the great magician."

"How much is it?" Ben asked.

Mr. Cream examined Ben for a few seconds. "Thirty dollars," he said. "Including tax."

Ben couldn't believe his luck. That's exactly what he had in his pocket. "I'll take it!" he said. Who needed the Official Junior Professional Magic Kit when he could buy a kit that once belonged to a famous magician? And now that he had a magic kit, he could quit his paper route.

Mr. Cream took the kit out of the window and handed it to Ben. "Use it wisely," he said. His green eyes seemed to see right through Ben.

"Sure," Ben said, handing him the money. "Uh, thanks!"

Ben ran all the way home before he realized he hadn't even looked inside the kit. That was weird. It was like something had come over him in the shop. He'd just known that he had to buy the kit.

Ben unlocked the back door and ran up to his room. His mom and dad wouldn't be home for another hour, so he'd have plenty of time to try out the kit. He just hoped there was something inside.

Ben sat on his bed and lifted the lid. A musty smell reached his nose. The kit contained three items: a black wand with a white tip, a black top hat, and an old book titled *Dr. Presto's Magic Spells*.

Ben frowned. He had been expecting a lot more, like some cool gimmicks to do tricks with. He picked up the book. He had never seen one like it in the library. Maybe it had instructions for creating illusions.

Ben flipped open the book to a page titled "Pulling a Rabbit from a Hat." The yellowed page was spotted with brown water stains, but Ben could make out most of the spell:

Hold the wand over the hat and
  repeat these words thrice:
Rabbitus physicalis!
Then tap the hat with the wand.

It didn't make sense. Everyone knew that to
make a rabbit appear out of a hat you needed a
live rabbit and a hat with a hidden compartment.
He examined the top hat from top to bottom. It
looked like an ordinary hat.

Still, the kit did belong to the great Dr. Presto.
Maybe there was some kind of magnetic device in
the wand that released a hidden spring in the hat.
Then some cardboard rabbit would pop out. It
was worth a try, anyway.

There was only one problem: Ben wasn't
exactly sure what "thrice" meant. He was pretty
sure it was a fancy word for a number. But was it
three or thirteen? He couldn't remember.

Oh well. It probably didn't matter. It wouldn't
matter if he got it wrong—would it?

If Ben says the magic words three times, go to page 8.

If Ben says the magic words thirteen times, go to page 12.

Continued from page 7

I'll say the words three times and then tap the wand on the hat, Ben decided. *If I get it wrong, I can always try thirteen times next.*

Ben put the hat on his lap and picked up the wand. He felt a little silly, but at least no one was watching him. He took a deep breath. "Rabbitus physicalus. Rabbitus physicalus. Rabbitus physicalus!" Ben said, getting louder each time he said the words. Then he tapped the hat with the wand.

Poof! A small cloud of gray smoke erupted from the hat, stinging Ben's eyes. The smoke cleared, and Ben gasped.

Inside the hat was a white rabbit! Ben carefully reached out and touched the rabbit's soft fur. The rabbit twitched its nose.

It was alive.

"No way," Ben whispered. It was impossible.

Ben picked up the rabbit and set it down on his bed. Then he examined the hat again. He ran his fingers over every inch of black felt. He pulled at every seam. He shook the hat as hard as he could. There was no sign of a hidden compartment anywhere.

Ben tapped the hat with the wand again. If the

hand was somehow mechanically connected to the hat, it shouldn't matter if he said the spell or not.

Nothing happened.

This couldn't be. Everything Ben had ever read or learned about magic had taught him that there was an explanation for every illusion ever performed. Magic was not real. Magicians simply did not make things appear out of thin air.

That weird Sebastian Cream guy must be behind this. Ben just knew it. He pulled out the business card, but there was no address or phone number listed. He ran downstairs and called information.

"Sorry, sir," the operator said. "We have no listing for Sebastian Cream's Curiosity Shop."

Ben put down the phone. No one was going to believe this, especially not his parents. He really wanted to talk to his friend Lori, but he knew Friday night was always family night at her house. He'd have to wait until morning.

Ben passed the time by fixing up a box for the rabbit and flipping through *Dr. Presto's Magic Spells*. Every page was the same. There were no instructions for creating tricks, just magic words and a lot of wand-tapping.

Ben dreamed of white rabbits all night. When he woke up, he got dressed, grabbed the rabbit's box, and ran next door.

Lori was in the backyard, feeding her own rabbits, Bugs and Peter. They lived in a wood-and-wire hutch in the yard. Lori was wearing jeans, like she always did, and a T-shirt from her karate school. She wore her red hair in two long braids.

Lori's eyes lit up when she saw that Ben was carrying a rabbit. "What a cute bunny!" she said, holding it up to her face.

"I was hoping you wouldn't mind taking care of it," Ben said. "It was, uh, kind of a surprise."

"What do you mean?" Lori asked. "Where did you get it?"

Ben told Lori the whole story.

"That's the craziest thing I ever heard," she said when Ben finished.

"I know," Ben said. "But it's true, I swear."

Lori put the rabbit in the hutch with Bugs and Peter. "Let's take a look at this magic kit," she said.

Ben got the magic kit out of his room and brought it outside. He and Lori sat on the front steps while Lori examined the contents.

"There has got to be a hidden compartment somewhere in this hat," Lori said.

"That's what I thought," Ben said. "But I couldn't find one."

"Hey, Houdini!" a voice called out. "What do you have there?"

It was Skip Feeney, the mailman. Ben usually had a trick or two to perform for Skip when he saw him. Skip was a great audience.

"It's a new magic kit," Ben said.

Skip sat down on the steps. "Cool!" he said. "Can you try one for me?"

He grabbed the book from Ben and began flipping through the pages. "Hey look!" he said, "Here's one. 'How to Make a Person Disappear.' Let's try it! You can make me disappear."

"I don't know," Ben said. "This kit is a little weird. I don't know if I should be using you like a guinea pig."

"I don't mind," Skip said. "Come on, it'll be fun."

"It would be a good experiment," Lori said.

Ben wasn't sure what to do. Something didn't feel quite right. Experimenting with another trick wasn't a bad idea—but maybe he should try the trick on himself instead.

If Ben tries to make Skip disappear, go to page 28.

If Ben tries to make himself disappear, go to page 15.

Continued from page 7

Ben thought about it. Thirteen was supposed to be some kind of magical number, right? He'd try saying the words thirteen times.

"Rabbitus physicalis! Rabbitus physicalus! Rabbitus physicalus . . . Rabbitus physicalus! . . . Rabbitus physicalis! . . . " It seemed to take forever. When he finished, he tapped the hat with the wand.

Nothing happened.

"Rats!" Ben cried. He threw the hat on the floor in frustration. "Why did I waste my time? I should have known it wouldn't work."

But Ben didn't usually give up so easily. He figured he could at least try doing the spell the other way. Maybe it would work this time. It was worth a shot. He reached down to pick up the hat.

And then he saw it.

There was a giant eye outside his window! A giant pink eye was looking in at him!

Ben stood frozen with fear. He stared out the window. The eye moved. Now Ben could make out a giant pink nose. A white furry face. Then a long, furry ear.

"A giant rabbit!" Ben whispered out loud. Ben rubbed his own eyes. "I-I can't believe it!"

The spell had worked. Sort of. Instead of a cute white bunny, Ben had conjured up a huge rabbit.

It's probably because I said the words thirteen times instead of three, Ben realized. *Rats!*

The rabbit hopped away from the window. Ben grabbed the magic book and stuffed it into his back pocket. Then he ran downstairs as fast as he could.

Breathless, Ben reached his backyard, slamming the door behind him. The giant rabbit was busy munching on the rosebushes.

Ben still couldn't believe what he was seeing. The rabbit looked kind of like a normal rabbit, only bigger. But this rabbit didn't look warm and cuddly. No. The rabbit looked sinister. Ben could see that its front and back legs were bulging with huge muscles. Two sharp-looking teeth jutted from the rabbit's mouth. A shiver ran down Ben's spine. He knew that those teeth could easily snap him in two!

Except for the munching sounds of the rabbit, Ben realized the neighborhood was quiet. That was good. Maybe nobody had noticed the rabbit yet. If they had, they'd be running like crazy from it. Ben knew that that was what he should be doing. But he also knew that he was probably the only one who could get rid of this crazy rabbit. All he had to do was cast a spell.

Ben took the book out of his pocket and flipped through it. There had to be something there.

Suddenly Ben heard a loud thud. He looked up. The rabbit had eaten every single rose in the garden. It hopped away, stomping on the wood fence that separated his house from his friend Lori's house next door.

"Hey, wait!" Ben called after it.

But the rabbit didn't listen. It hopped down the driveway.

Ben started to run after it. Then he stopped.

No one knows I did this, he thought. *If they find out, I'll be in big trouble. Maybe I should just let animal control handle it. It's really not my problem anymore. But then again, I'm probably the only one who can fix this mess.*

If Ben lets the rabbit go, go to page 82.

If Ben decides to try to stop the rabbit, go to page 32.

"Sorry, Skip," Ben said. "It's too dangerous."

Skip shrugged. "Okay. But I'll be back same time Monday if you want to try."

Lori shook her head. "I can't believe you think that kit is really magic," she said. "That's not like, you, Ben."

"I don't believe the kit is magic," Ben said. "But until I know for sure, I don't want to take any chances. At least not with anyone else."

Ben looked at the spell:

Hold the wand over the subject's head. Then say these words:
Exvanire, disapparensis, departire!

That sounded easy enough. He stood up and held the wand over his head.

"Here goes," he said. Then he repeated the words in the spell. "Exvanire, disapparensis, departire!"

Poof! A cloud of gray smoke exploded in front of his face. Ben coughed and tried to fan away the smoke with his free hand. "See, Lori?" he said, when the smoke cleared. "Nothing hap—"

Ben froze. Lori wasn't there anymore.

Neither were his front steps. Or his house.

Or the world.

Ben let out a long breath and looked around. The sky above him, if you could call it a sky, was completely white. The ground below him was made up of black-and-white squares. The pattern extended in all directions as far as he could see. "What is this place?" Ben asked out loud. He realized then that he still held the magic wand in his hand.

Ben turned in a circle, hoping to find some sign of life—anything. In the distance something caught his eye. A white post was sticking out of the ground. He stuck the wand in his back pocket and walked toward it.

Ben's feet made no sound as he walked across the checkerboard ground. As he got closer, he saw an arrow on top of the post. Painted on the arrow were the words THIS WAY OUT.

Ben had no idea what was happening. His best guess was that the kit was some kind of virtual-reality device. It must be tricking him into thinking he was in this weird place. If he followed the sign, hopefully the trick would end.

"I wouldn't do that if I were you," someone said.

Ben looked in the direction of the voice. He didn't see anyone.

"Down here."

Ben looked down. At his feet was a white rabbit. The rabbit was standing on its hind legs, its pink eyes fixed on Ben. "The sign is a trick," she said. "Follow me. I will show you how to leave here safely."

Ben closed his eyes and opened them again. Nope. The talking rabbit was still there. Could he trust it?

If Ben follows the rabbit, go to page 36.

If Ben follows the sign, go to page 68.

Continued from page 27

Ben didn't think he could outrun the soldiers. He'd need a diversion first. The rabbits just might work.

Ben set the hat on the ground. He repeated the words from the rabbit spell thirteen times:

"Rabbitus physicalus!"

Then he tapped the hat with the wand.

Poof! went the cloud of smoke, and a giant white rabbit appeared in the warehouse, crushing the hat underneath it. Fuller and the soldiers stared at the rabbit in amazement. Then they all began to talk at once.

Ben took advantage of the confusion to sneak up to the rabbit. "Rabbitus multiplicatus!" he whispered.

Then he ran.

Giant rabbits burst from nowhere, causing havoc in the lab. Machines crashed to the ground. Smoke poured from electrical devices. The soldiers ran around the warehouse after the rabbits, bumping into one another in confusion.

In the center of it all stood Maximillian Fuller, pulling on the ends of his hair. "This wasn't supposed to happen!" he screamed.

Ben didn't stay long enough to see anymore.

The hat was crushed, but he had the wand and the book. The giant rabbits were Fuller's problem now.

Ben ran home and found Lori on his front steps, holding the empty magic kit. Ben stuffed the wand and the book inside. He couldn't keep the magic kit anymore. It was too dangerous. But he knew one place where it would be safe. "I'll be back soon," he told Lori. "I've got to go back to Sebastian Cream's Curiosity Shop."

Go to page 137.

Continued from page 49

"Hurry up!" Lori wailed.

Ben threw down the book. He might as well try saying the spell backward. At least it would be fast. "Antigravitus levitatus!" he cried.

Ben hoped Lori would come crashing down to the floor, but that didn't happen. She was still floating in the air.

"Do you feel any different?" he asked Lori.

Lori's face had turned pale. "Nope," she replied. "But I bet you do."

"What do you mean?" Ben asked.

Suddenly, Ben had a strange feeling. Something wasn't right. He looked down at his feet.

They weren't touching the floor!

"Oh no," Ben said. "What have I done?"

"Well, it looks like you didn't reverse the spell," Lori said. "You made yourself levitate!"

Ben could feel his body getting lighter and lighter. He tried to reach down to grab the book of spells, but he was too far away.

"Ben, watch out!" Lori yelled.

Ben turned around. His bedroom window was open. "Help!" he cried out to Lori.

But she couldn't help. Desperately Ben tried to

reach for something to hold on to. He grabbed for the windowsill. But a gust of wind kicked up, and Ben lost his grip. The wind carried him up, up, and away . . . like a lost balloon.

"Help!" Ben screamed again, but he was higher than the trees now. No one could hear him.

Only the birds.

THE END

Continued from page 89

Ben tried to focus. Which dove was it?

His instinct had been to go to the dove in the round cage. Maybe he'd better trust his instinct.

Besides, if I'm wrong, Ben thought, *what's the worst that could happen? I mean, how much danger could a little itty-bitty dove lead me into?*

"Here goes nothing," Ben said. He opened the door of the round cage.

For a moment the dove did nothing.

Ben held his breath.

Then the dove flew out of the cage.

"Thank you," the dove said, hovering in front of Ben's face.

"Great!" Ben said, breathing a big sigh of relief. "Let's get out of here."

Ben started to go. But the dove just hovered in place.

Suddenly the dove's pink eyes began to glow with an eerie red light.

"Uh-oh," Ben said.

Ben watched, stunned, as the white dove began to transform. Its body grew larger. Its wings transformed into two human arms. Its wiry legs turned into human legs.

A magician in a white tuxedo was standing before Ben.

"Cool!" Ben said. "So can we get out of here now?"

The magician smiled an evil smile. "Only one of us will be getting out of here," he said with an evil-looking grin. "And it won't be you!"

The magician pulled a white wand out of his pocket. He pointed it at Ben. "Transformus aviarus!"

Ben felt the wave of magic hit his body. Then everything began to change. He could feel his body shrinking . . . his arms sprouting feathers . . . his nose and mouth transforming. "What's going on?" Ben asked, but his voice came out like a squeak.

Ben felt himself being lifted up. He was face-to-face with the magician. And he was standing in the palm of the magician's hand! What was happening?

Ben tried to speak, but again, nothing except squeaks came out.

"Someone must take my place," the magician said. Then he put Ben inside the golden cage and closed the door.

Ben panicked. What had the magician done to him?

He looked down at his body. White feathers

covered every inch of his skin. His arms were two wide wings. His legs were skinny bird feet.

Then it hit him.

"I'm a dove!" he shrieked.

The magician laughed, a loud laugh that bounced off of the walls of the room. Then he walked through the wall and disappeared.

The dove in the square cage looked at Ben. "You should have picked me!" she said.

THE END

Continued from page 92

This guy is more like a mad *scientist*, Ben thought. *First, giant bunnies. Now a mad scientist. What next?*

"I have been studying the science of magic for decades," Fuller continued. "Years ago, I discovered an interesting secret about a magician named Dr. Presto. Instead of creating illusions with wires and mirrors, it was said that he possessed ancient secrets. I made it my life's work to possess those secrets.

"I even found Presto's journal. In it he talked about a magic kit that contained all of his power. I searched for years to find it, but never could," Fuller said. "Then tonight, I saw a news report about giant rabbits in the Bleaktown gardens. I immediately dispatched my soldiers to investigate. And they brought me these." He held up the hat and the wand.

"What are you going to do?" Ben asked.

"What do you think?" Fuller asked. "With Dr. Presto's magic, I can rule the world!"

Oh great, Ben thought groaning.

Fuller put the top hat on his head. It teetered on top of his bushy hair. He waved the wand in front of him. "Let the magic begin!" he said dramatically. "Abracadabra!"

25

Ben tried not to laugh. He had seen enough of Dr. Presto's book to know that the word "abra-cadabra" wasn't anywhere in sight. All of the spells were written in some kind of old language, like Latin or something.

Then a sudden thought caused Ben to freeze with fear. The book was still in his back pocket. Fuller might look pretty silly now, but if he got hold of the book, he could be dangerous. Ben couldn't let him have it—no matter what. He glanced around the lab, searching for a way out.

"Abracadabra! Abracadabra!" Fuller shouted, becoming more and more angry.

Ben spotted a fire exit on the far wall. He began to inch toward it. "Well, good luck with the ruling-the-world thing," he said casually. "I'll get out of your way now."

"Stop!" Fuller shouted. He pointed the wand at Ben. "You must know how these tools of magic work. You used them to create the giant rabbits, didn't you?"

"Who, me?" Ben said innocently.

Fuller leaned down and stuck his skinny nose in Ben's face. "Tell me the secrets of Dr. Presto," he said. "Or you will pay!"

Ben thought quickly. "I don't remember what I did exactly," he said. "Maybe if you give me the hat and the wand I can remember."

Fuller's eyes narrowed. "I'm not a fool. You could be tricking me."

Ben tried to look as innocent as possible. "I'm just a dumb kid. You're a mad—I mean, brilliant scientist. How could I trick you?"

The flattery worked. Fuller handed Ben the hat and the wand. "Now show me," he demanded.

Ben thought about what to do. Now that he had the hat and the wand, he could try to make a run for it.

But he could also use the hat and wand to cast a spell. But the only spell he knew was how to make giant rabbits. How would that be any help?

If Ben decides to cast a spell, go to page 18.

If Ben decides to run for it, go to page 55.

Continued from page 11

Ben snapped to his senses. He knew that it was impossible to create the illusion of a vanishing person with just a wand and a hat. You needed a false wall or a cabinet with a hidden compartment. Nothing bad was going to happen to Skip. It was impossible.

"All right, Skip," Ben said. "Let's try this!"

Ben put the hat on his head and looked at the spell:

> **Hold the wand over the subject's head.**
> **Then say these words:**
> **Exvanire, disapparensis, departire!**

Ben picked up the wand. "Why don't you stand over there, Skip?" Ben pointed to the tree in his front yard.

Ben followed Skip to the tree. He reached up and held the wand over the mailman's head.

"Hey, aren't you going to, you know, talk up the trick before you do it?" Skip asked. "Build up suspense and everything?"

"We're just practicing," Ben said. "Besides, I don't even think anything's going to happen."

Skip looked disappointed.

Ben read from the book. "Exvanire,

disaparensis, departire!"

Poof! A cloud of smoke exploded in front of Skip. Goose bumps popped up on Ben's skin. This looked too familiar.

The smoke cleared.

And Skip was nowhere in sight.

"Oh man," Ben said. He turned to Lori. "See! I told you there was something weird about this kit!"

Lori walked up to Ben. Then she walked all around the tree.

"This doesn't prove anything," she said. "Skip could have ducked behind the tree when the smoke appeared. He's probably just playing a trick on you."

Lori had to be right. Skip could not have vanished into thin air.

Still, the whole thing left him with a creepy feeling.

"That doesn't explain how the smoke appeared," Ben pointed out.

"There's probably something in the wand that gets activated when it taps something," Lori said.

Ben tapped the wand on the tree. No smoke came out.

"Skip!" Ben called out. "Very funny, Skip. You can come out now."

But Skip was still nowhere in sight.

"This is *really* giving me the creeps," Ben told Lori.

"Don't worry, Ben. I mean, there's no *way* Skip could have *really* vanished, right? You'll see, Skip'll show up here Monday to deliver the mail, just like usual."

"Yeah," Ben said. "Skip's pretty goofy. He's probably just trying to freak me out or something."

"Of course," Lori said. "Do you want to try another trick?"

Ben looked at Dr. Presto's face peering from the black bag and shivered. "No thanks," he said. "I've had enough magic for one day."

Ben spent the rest of the day helping to take care of Lori's rabbits and playing his favorite video game. That night, he dreamed of white rabbits in mailman uniforms. But when he woke up, the sun was streaming through the window. The smell of bacon was wafting up from the kitchen. Everything seemed perfectly normal. Ben smiled and got dressed. Then, like he did every Sunday morning, he walked out to the front lawn to get the paper for his mom and dad.

The newspaper carrier had tossed the paper into a bush. Ben shook his head. Those weekend carriers were always in such a hurry. Ben plucked the paper out of the bushes.

Then Ben went cold. The front page headline seemed to leap out of the pages at him.

BLEAKTOWN MAIL CARRIER MISSING

Ben sank down onto the steps and read the story. Apparently Skip Feeney had not returned from his mail route yesterday. His mom had called the police, and they were investigating.

Ben ran to Lori's house and banged on the door. She answered in her pajamas. Her red braids were sticking out in two different directions.

"Look at this!" Ben said, thrusting the paper into her hands.

Lori read the article. "This must be part of Skip's joke," she said. "And if it isn't, then it's not your fault. You do not have the power to make people disappear!"

"Maybe *I* don't," Ben said. "But the kit does."

"Let's solve this once and for all," Lori said. "Try out another trick on me."

"No way," Ben said. "It's too dangerous. I'm going to look for Skip!"

If Ben agrees to try out a trick on Lori, go to page 46.

If Ben decides to go look for Skip, go to page 58.

Continued from page 14

Letting the rabbit go was tempting. But Ben just couldn't do it. He had made it appear, and it was his responsibility to take care of it. That's what Harry Houdini would have done.

Ben thought quickly. He'd have to trap the rabbit somewhere. The garage would be perfect. Luckily the rabbit was distracted by a hydrangea bush growing on the side of the house.

Ben found the garage remote control in its hiding place under a rock. He opened the garage. Then he bravely stepped up to the rabbit.

"Hey, rabbit!" Ben called out. "I've got some more roses for you."

The rabbit stopped munching the hydrangeas. It turned to Ben. Its big pink nose twitched curiously.

Ben wasn't sure if the rabbit would understand him, but he thought it was worth a try. It was a magic rabbit, after all.

"They're in there," Ben said, pointing to the garage. "Lots of them. They're really tasty, too. Mmmmm."

The rabbit turned toward the garage. Its nose twitched again, as though searching for the smell of roses.

"They're way in the back," Ben said. "You should go see them. It's worth it."

The rabbit seemed to believe Ben's story. It hopped toward the garage. Ben dodged to the side as the rabbit's fur grazed past him. It was all he could do to keep from running away, screaming.

The rabbit squeezed into the garage, its fuzzy tail facing Ben. Ben hit the button on the remote, and the door slowly closed.

The rabbit made some furious chattering sounds, but the space was too tight for it to turn around. The door closed all the way, trapping the rabbit inside.

Ben breathed a sigh of relief. But his problem wasn't solved yet. He needed help.

Ben ran next door and pounded on the back door of his friend Lori's house. Lori came to the door wearing jeans, sneakers, and a T-shirt from her karate school. Her red hair hung in two long braids down her back. She looked annoyed. "Ben, you know tonight is family night," she said. "We're playing Monopoly. I own Boardwalk!"

"It's an emergency, Lori," Ben pleaded. "Please! It's serious."

"What kind of emergency?" Lori asked.

Ben pointed to the garage. The rabbit's giant fluffy tail wiggled back and forth against the glass windows.

"Okay," Lori said. "I'll be right back."

Lori appeared a few seconds later. She and Ben walked into his driveway.

"So is that really a giant rabbit in your garage?" Lori asked.

"Uh-huh," Ben replied. He told her about his visit to Sebastian Cream's Curiosity Shop and Dr. Presto's magic kit.

"This is too weird," Lori said. "But it must be true. So what are you going to do now?"

Ben showed Lori the book. "I thought there might be something in here," he said. "I didn't have time to look before."

He and Lori sat on the ground and opened the book. The rabbit was making strange, loud noises inside the garage. It sounded like it was slamming against the walls.

"We'd better hurry," Lori said.

"Right," Ben agreed.

There was no table of contents in the book, so she turned every page. Finally Lori spotted something. "Here's a shrinking spell," she said. "Maybe you could use that to make the rabbit small again. You've got to say some words and tap the rabbit with the wand."

"That sounds good," Ben said. "But I'm not sure I want to get that close to the rabbit. Let's see if there's anything else."

Ben turned the pages until he noticed a black-and-white drawing of a rabbit. The words "Rabbitus multiplicatus" were written underneath it. But the top of the page was torn off. Ben wasn't sure what the spell was for.

"This could be it," Ben said. "At least we know it's about rabbits."

"So we've got two choices," Lori said. "Which spell do you want to try?"

If Ben tries the shrinking spell, go to page 129.

If Ben tries the rabbit spell, go to page 61.

Ben thought about what to do. Rabbits were cute and cuddly creatures. They wiggled their little noses and hopped around all day and ate carrots, right? How could he not trust a rabbit? "I'll follow you," Ben said.

The rabbit nodded and got down on four legs. "Stick to the black squares," it called. "They will lead the way."

Ben followed the rabbit as it hopped from black square to black square. It moved quickly, and it wasn't easy to keep up.

"So what is this place, anyway?" Ben asked as they hopped. "Some kind of virtual-reality program?"

The rabbit stopped and turned to Ben. "I assure you that everything here is real. *Very* real," it said. "We are in the land of Magic Limbo." It turned around and started hopping again.

"Magic Limbo?" Ben asked. "What kind of place is that?"

The rabbit slowed its pace a little. "Magic Limbo is the land where things go when magicians make them disappear," it explained to Ben.

"You mean, when a magician makes his assistant disappear, she comes *here*?" Ben asked.

"That's right," the rabbit replied. "And flowers. And doves. And scarves. And—"

"Rabbits, of course," Ben put in. "But I don't understand something. Things can't get stuck in Magic Limbo *forever*, can they? I mean, magicians pull rabbits and scarves and doves and other things *out* of their hats. So they have to reappear sometime, right?"

The rabbit nodded its head. "That's just it," it said. "Only the *magician* can cause the object to appear in the real world."

Ben thought about this a minute. Then he stopped on a square. "Wait!" he called out.

The rabbit stopped and twitched its whiskers.

"*I* made myself disappear," he said. "I mean, there's no magician on the other side who can bring me back."

The rabbit wiggled its ears impatiently. "I know that," it said. "But you do have your wand with you. The wand can bring you home. But there is not much time."

It didn't make sense. Magicians didn't *really* make things disappear. It just looked that way.

But he was here, wasn't he? That had to prove something.

Suddenly the checkerboard floor ended. Beyond it was white empty space. The rabbit stopped hopping.

Before them stood a black ladder. It rose as far up as Ben could see and also led down as far as Ben could see.

"This is as far as I can go," the rabbit said. Then it hurried away. "You can take it from here."

"Wait!" Ben called after her. "Am I supposed to go up or down?"

If Ben goes up the ladder, go to page 52.

If Ben goes down the ladder, go to page 64.

Continued from page 63

Ben had no time to think. When he reached the end of the street, he turned left.

As soon as he made the turn, he found himself in a small alleyway. And the alleyway dead-ended into a high brick wall!

"No!" Ben cried.

Quickly he turned around and came face-to-face with the rabbits! Their giant furry bodies blocked the alley. There was no way out.

The rabbits came closer and closer to Ben.

"Nice bunnies," he said, backing up slowly.

The rabbits kept on hopping. Their pink noses twitched. Their muscles bulged. As they got closer, Ben could see that each one of their teeth was twice as big as his own head.

Thwack! Ben collided against the brick wall. This was it. There was nowhere else to go. He was trapped!

Then Ben remembered the book in his back pocket. This was his only hope—his only way out! Ben reached into his pocket to grab the book.

But it was gone! Frantically Ben patted his other pocket. Nothing. The book must have fallen out when he ran.

"Nice bunnies," Ben said again, trying to

sound friendly. "I'm sure we can work something out."

The rabbits were not impressed. They charged toward Ben, their ears twitching wildly.

And they looked hungry.

Very hungry.

THE END

Continued from page 81

Dr. Presto's offer impressed Ben. If he was trained by the great Dr. Presto, he could grow up to be the greatest magician in the world. He imagined the cheering crowds . . . the television specials . . . the big paychecks.

This was a dream come true!

"That sounds great, Dr. Presto," Ben said. "When can we start?"

Lori grabbed Ben's sleeve. "What is going on here, Ben? Did you really disappear? Is this really Dr. Presto? And what is that Magic Limbo place all about? Come on, Ben. What's the deal?"

"It's all real, Lori," Ben said. "I really disappeared and I went to this place called Magic Limbo. And Dr. Presto is the real thing, too. Right, Dr. Presto?"

"What my friend Ben says is correct," Dr. Presto replied. "Why don't we start your first lesson right now?"

"Sure, Dr. Presto!" Ben said eagerly.

"I-I don't know about this," Lori interrupted.

"Don't worry," Ben said. "This is going to be great. You'll see. Maybe Dr. Presto will even show you a few things, Lori." Ben turned to Dr. Presto. "Where do you want to study?" he asked.

41

"Right here is fine," the magician said. "But of course I'll need the proper tools. Besides the wand, there were a book and a hat in my magic kit. Do you have them?"

Ben had left everything on the steps when he vanished into Magic Limbo. He gathered them up and handed them to the magician.

"And the wand, of course," Dr. Presto said.

Ben hesitated just a second. The last time he gave up the wand, Dr. Presto had turned on him. He didn't know what to do, but Dr. Presto really seemed like he wanted to teach him.

Dr. Presto seemed to read Ben's mind. "You can trust me, Ben. I can't teach you without my tools."

Ben handed over the wand.

Dr. Presto smiled. "And now for the first lesson," he said.

"What are you going to teach me?" Ben asked.

A shadow crossed Dr. Presto's face. "Never trust a magician who has tricked you once already."

Ben's stomach flip-flopped. "What do you mean?" he asked.

"This wand was the only way to escape from Magic Limbo," he said. "Thank you for bringing it to me. But now I am free, and you and your little friend know too much. I'm afraid I have to

send you where you can't do me any harm.
Exvanire, disapparensis, departire!"

Poof! Smoke filled the air. Ben shut his eyes.
He was pretty sure what he would see when he
opened them.

"Ben! Where are we?" Lori cried.

Ben opened his eyes. The checkerboard floor
stretched out in all directions around them.
Sitting on one black square was a white rabbit.

"I told you so!" said the rabbit.

THE END

Continued from page 107

Normally the idea of jumping onto a garbage truck would seem crazy to Ben. He had never even used a skateboard. But right now, this seemed like the best solution.

The garbage truck breezed past, and Ben jumped up and grabbed the ladder. He rested his feet on the bottom rung.

Ben held on to the ladder with one hand. In his other hand, he grasped the hat.

The garbage truck picked up speed, and the soldiers let out a cry behind him. Ben held on tightly as the truck careened around the corner.

Ben soon figured out that the truck had made all of its stops for the day and was heading back to the dump. Luckily it looked as though the truck would take him close to his house.

The soldiers couldn't keep up. Ben was glad he had jumped onto the truck. He waited until the soldiers were completely out of sight and got off when the truck stopped for a stop sign. Then he raced home.

As he reached his front steps, he saw Lori sitting there. She held the empty magic kit in her hands.

"What in the world happened to you?" Lori asked.

Ben quickly explained what had happened. Then he put the wand, the hat, and the book back into the kit and locked it tightly. Ben knew what he had to do.

"Those soldiers said that someone was after the magic kit," he said. "This thing could be dangerous in the wrong hands. I'm going to take it back to Sebastian Cream's Curiosity Shop."

Go to page 137.

"Listen to yourself, Ben," Lori said. "You've been studying magic all these years. You know it's not real. And it's not dangerous. Just try a trick out on me. What could go wrong?"

"All right," Ben agreed giving in. "But nothing too complicated. I will definitely *not* try to saw you in half."

"Chicken," Lori said, grinning.

Ben went back to his room and waited for Lori to get ready. He flipped through the book and finally decided on a levitation spell. Nothing could go terribly wrong with that, right?

> *To make your assistant levitate:*
> *Instruct the assistant to lie down.*
> *Pass the wand over the assistant six times.*
> *Then say these words: Levitatus antigravitus!*
> *Your assistant will become as light as a*
> *feather and float in midair.*

It seemed harmless enough. Ben took the blanket and pillows from his bed and spread them out on the floor. If something weird did happen, and Lori really did end up flying, she'd have a safe place to land.

"Ready, Houdini?" Lori was at Ben's door.

"I think so," Ben said. "I found a levitation

spell. That's impossible to do without some kind of special pole or harness or wires. If you start floating, then this kit is definitely magic!"

Lori laughed. "Well, I really doubt anything will happen."

"We'll see," Be said with a shrug. "Why don't you lie down on the floor with your arms at your sides."

Lori did as Ben instructed and closed her eyes.

"Here goes," Ben said. He waved the wand over Lori six times. "Levitatus antigravitus!" Ben shouted.

Nothing happened.

"See?" Lori said. "I knew this kit wasn't really magic. Don't you feel better?"

But Ben couldn't answer her.

Lori's body should have been touching the floor. But it wasn't.

There was a half inch of space between Lori and the blanket. And the space was getting bigger every second.

"Uh, Lori," Ben said. "Do you feel—different?"

"Just hungry," Lori said. "I skipped breakfast. Why?"

Now Lori was even with the top of Ben's desk.

"Look down," Ben said.

"How can I look down? I am dow—whoa!" Laurie screamed. "I'm floating!"

47

"I know!" Ben said.

"Make it stop!" Lori cried. Then she bumped into the ceiling. "Ow!"

A horrible vision flashed through Ben's mind. Once, when he was five, he had won a red helium balloon at the carnival. But he let go of the balloon by mistake, and the balloon had floated away. Ben had watched it float higher and higher until it disappeared.

Is that what would happen to Lori?

"Hang on to something," Ben said. "I'll get you down."

"Make it fast!" Lori cried. She crawled across the ceiling and grabbed on to Ben's ceiling fan.

Ben grabbed Dr. Presto's book. There had to be a way to reverse the spell. He turned back to the levitation spell.

The page after it was yellowed with age, but Ben could make out one line. It said, "Repeat the spell backward."

Backward. That must be it. If he said the spell backward, he might be able to reverse the spell.

Then the book fell out of Ben's hands. It almost felt as if someone had pulled it away. Ben reached down to pick it up and saw that the book had opened up to a new spell: "In Case of Emergency."

Well, this was certainly an emergency. Ben

wasn't sure what to do. Should he try saying the spell backward, or use the emergency spell?

If Ben tries the emergency spell, go to page 72.
If Ben tries to reverse the spell, go to page 20.

Continued from page 71

Ben took a deep breath. He stepped on the left pedal.

Then he screamed.

The cabinet floor gave way underneath him. Ben felt himself falling. Down, down, down.

Thud! He finally landed on a hard white floor.

Ben looked around. He was in a small, white room. The white rabbit sat on the floor across from him.

"I told you so," said the rabbit.

Ben stared at the rabbit. "What are you talking about?" he asked.

"When Dr. Presto sent himself to Magic Limbo, he made one mistake," the rabbit said. "He forgot to bring his wand with him. He couldn't leave without the wand."

Ben groaned as he realized what had happened. "That's why he took the wand from me. It was a trick!"

The rabbit nodded its head.

"No problem," Ben said, rising to his feet. "You can show me the way out of here now."

The rabbit's nose twitched. "No, I can't."

"What do you mean, you can't?" Ben asked.

"Weren't you listening to what I said? You have

to have the wand to get out of Magic Limbo," she replied.

A cold chill crept over Ben. "So you mean . . ."

"You're trapped in Magic Limbo forever!"

THE END

Continued from page 38

Ben decided to climb up the ladder. The only thing he could see above him were soft clouds of swirling white mist.

After ten minutes of climbing, Ben began to feel nervous. What if he had made the wrong choice? This ladder seemed to be going nowhere.

Almost as soon as he had the thought, the mist parted. Ben saw a white ceiling above him. The ladder rose up through a hole in the ceiling. Ben took a deep breath and climbed through the hole.

And found himself staring into three faces!

Startled Ben almost lost his grip. An arm grabbed his, and he was pulled up onto the floor.

"We thought we lost you," said one of the rescuers, a boyish-looking guy wearing a bright yellow leotard.

"We sure don't get many visitors up here," said another, a pretty woman with white-blond hair that bobbed against her shoulders. She wore a red skirt and short, sequined jacket.

"Why would anyone come visit us? There's never anything happening up here," said the third, a tall woman with long, red hair. She wore a sleek black gown and long, black gloves.

Ben stood up. "Thanks for helping me. I'm

Ben," he said. "Is this the way out?"

All three stared at Ben like he was crazy. Then they burst out laughing.

"Sorry, kid," said the blonde. "There's no way out of here. You might as well make yourself comfortable."

The blonde waved her hand toward some red velvet couches in the center of the room.

"What do you mean there's no way out?" Ben asked, sitting on the couch.

The man in the yellow leotard looked at the two women. "We'd better tell him."

The women shrugged, and the man sat down next to Ben on the couch. "My name is Sparky," he began. "I used to be Dr. Presto's assistant."

"Hey, I've heard of you!" Ben exclaimed. "I read about you in *The Encyclopedia of Magicians*."

"Then you must know Ruby and Clarissa," Sparky said, pointing to the blonde and the redhead.

Ben couldn't believe it. These guys were famous in the world of magic. "What are you guys doing here?" he asked.

"Dr. Presto got tired of us, one by one," Clarissa said, sinking into the couch. "But instead of just firing us, he sent us all here, to Magic Limbo. He was afraid we would give up his secrets."

"And now we're stuck in this dump forever," Ruby said glumly.

Ben took the wand from his pocket. "That's not what the talking rabbit said. It said I could use this wand to get out of here."

The assistants' eyes lit up when they saw the wand. They crowded around Ben.

"Do you know what we could do with this?" Clarissa said, her green eyes gleaming.

"I just said, we can get out of here," Ben said. "And you guys can come with me."

The assistants looked at one another again and laughed.

"We do want to leave," Sparky said. "But we want something even more."

"What's that?" Ben asked.

"We want revenge on Dr. Presto!" Clarissa cried. "And we can use your wand to do it!"

The look on Clarissa's face was making Ben nervous. She looked almost . . . possessed. Maybe he should go back down the ladder before things got out of control.

If Ben goes back down the ladder, go to page 77.

If Ben helps the assistants get revenge on Dr. Presto, go to page 125.

Continued from page 27

Ben had had enough of giant rabbits and soldiers and mad scientists for one day. He decided to take his chances and run for it.

But he had to come up with a plan. And he knew it better be fast.

"You guys might want to stand back," Ben said, pointing his wand at Fuller and the soldiers. "The last time I did this, there was kind of an explosion."

It was a just a little lie, but it worked. Fuller and the soldiers stepped back. Good. That gave Ben plenty of room to put his plan into action. He put the hat on his head and waved the wand in the air. "Meus escapus!" Ben cried.

"Meus escapus? What does that mean?" Fuller asked.

"It means—" Ben didn't finish. He darted to the right, passing by the stunned soldiers.

"Stop him!" Fuller yelled.

But Ben had taken them by surprise. He ran through the fire exit and tore down the street without looking back.

After several blocks Ben realized he did not hear anyone following him. He collapsed on the grass, exhausted. They must have given up.

A bug hopped on Ben's head. He reached up to slap it.

That's when he realized that the hat was gone.

"I must have dropped it when I was running," Ben said. And then it hit him.

He wasn't holding the wand, either.

"That's okay," Ben said. "I've still got the book."

He reached into his back pocket.

The book was gone too.

Ben groaned. He must have lost the hat, the wand, and the book in his hurry. That's why the soldiers weren't chasing him. Fuller hadn't gotten Ben to show him any magic tricks, but now he had the book, the hat, and the wand.

He thought about going to the warehouse to try to stop Fuller, but decided against it. He was just one kid. What could he do against a mad scientist and all those soldiers?

Besides, he didn't think Fuller could *really* rule the world. He turned away and started to walk home.

Just then, a Ben heard a low rumbling sound. It was still sunny out, so Ben didn't think it was going to rain. He looked up at the sky. Suddenly a dark shadow crossed over the bright sun. Ben froze in his tracks.

Maximillian Fuller towered over Bleaktown.

His bushy hair stuck out over the tops of the town's tallest trees. "No one tricks Maximillian Fuller!" the mad scientist bellowed.

Ben sighed and got back on his feet. There was only one thing left to do.

Run!

THE END

Continued from page 31

Ben went back home and grabbed the magic kit. If Skip was in some kind of trouble, he might be able to use the kit to help. He told his parents he was going for a walk and headed out to look for Skip.

Skip and his mom lived downtown in an apartment that was next to the post office. Skip always used to joke that he had grown up next to the post office, and he dreamed about become a mail carrier since he could remember. He was so happy when his dream came true.

Poor Skip, Ben thought as he hurried downtown. *I will find you. I promise!*

Ben ran down Maple Street, a pretty, tree-lined street that was home to some of the largest houses in Bleaktown. The houses all had neat front lawns dotted with colorful flowers.

Ben was about to turn the corner when he noticed something. A white wooden sign had been erected on the front lawn of a large house on the corner. The house boasted a new coat of bright purple paint. The sign read: THE BLEAKTOWN HOME FOR RETIRED MAGICIANS.

Ben couldn't believe his luck. The home must have just opened. Now here was a whole house full of magicians who might be able to help him. He walked up the steps and knocked on the heavy wooden door.

There was no reply. But the door slowly creaked open by itself.

Weird, Ben thought. *Maybe it's just the magicians showing off.* He pushed the door open farther and stepped inside.

The door opened into a dark hallway. An archway on the right led the way to a large, open room.

Ben stepped toward the room. It was some kind of parlor. The room was filled with old men wearing ragged and patched tuxedos. As Ben looked around the room, he noticed that one of the old men wore a clean white tuxedo and a ruby red silk tie. He was performing a card trick for some of the other men. They looked tired and bored, as though they had seen it all before.

Ben stepped into the room. "Excuse me," he said, raising his voice. "I need some advice about this magic kit I just bought. Can anyone here help me?"

Ben held up the kit. Some of the magicians gasped. A few quickly left the room.

The magician in the white tuxedo stepped toward Ben, smiling. He had a skinny mustache that Ben guessed had been dyed black. His eyes were locked onto the magic kit. "Is that Dr. Presto's magic kit you have there?" he asked.

"Uh-huh," Ben replied.

The magician bowed. "Allow me to introduce myself," he said. "I am Mr. Mysterioso, Magician Extraordinaire. I will be happy to help you. It's a marvelous kit."

"Thanks!" Ben said gratefully. Maybe now he could finally help Skip.

"Do not listen to that charlatan!" someone growled.

Ben turned toward the voice. It came from an old magician in the corner. His once-black tuxedo was now a dingy gray. The knees and elbows were patched.

"I am Garfield the Great," the man said, standing up. "You cannot trust Mr. Mysterioso. Let *me* help you with the kit. It's dangerous in the wrong hands."

Ben wasn't sure what to do. Mr. Mysterioso looked a lot more professional than Garfield the Great. But appearances could be deceiving.

If Ben lets Garfield the Great help him, go to page 84.

If Ben lets Mr. Mysterioso help him, go to page 100.

Continued from page 35

Ben could not face getting close enough to the giant rabbit to tap it with the wand. He decided to try the other spell instead.

Half of the page was missing, so Ben wasn't exactly sure what to do. He put the top hat on his head. Then he pointed the wand at the rabbit and said the words aloud: "Rabbitus multiplicatus!"

Boom!

The garage seemed to explode in front of them. Lori tackled Ben, who stood frozen in his spot. They flew out of the driveway and landed on the soft grass in Ben's backyard.

"What happened?" Ben asked, dazed.

The giant rabbit hopped through the rubble of the broken garage.

And then another giant rabbit hopped after it.

And another.

And another.

And another.

"You made more rabbits!" Lori cried.

Ben sprang to his feet. The rabbits had reached the end of the driveway and were turning onto the street. If they kept going, they'd reach downtown in just a few minutes.

"I've got to stop them," Ben said. He spotted

the book on the driveway. It was squished, but all right. He stashed it in his pocket.

Lori stood up, then winced in pain.

"My ankle," she said. "I think I sprained it when we fell."

Ben had no choice. He had to go alone. "Sorry, Lori. I gotta go. I'll be back as soon as I can." He took off after the rabbits.

Luckily the rabbits seemed to be more interested in eating than anything else right now. They were distracted by the bushes growing on his neighbor's front lawn. But he knew it wouldn't last for long.

Ben ran in front of the rabbits and waved his wand to get their attention. "Hey, bunnies!" he yelled. "Bet you can't catch me!"

Ten giant rabbit ears twitched. Five pairs of pink eyes turned in Ben's direction.

And then the rabbits began to hop.

Ben turned and ran as fast as he could. The rabbits' pounding feet sounded like thunder.

Panic caused Ben's thoughts to bounce around his brain like Ping-Pong balls. But a plan managed to make its way through.

The Bleaktown city garden wasn't far away at all. If Ben could get the rabbits there, there would be enough plants and flowers to keep them busy for a while. It would give him enough time to look in the book again and to try another spell to get rid of the rabbits for good. It was his only hope.

Now Ben just had to remember how to get there. When he reached the end of his block, he made a right turn onto Maple Street. So far so good.

He snuck a quick look behind him. The rabbits were catching up, but he was still safe. All those weeks of delivering papers up steep hills had been great training.

Up ahead Ben saw that Maple Street was about to come to an end. There was a T-shaped intersection.

The gardens. The gardens. Ben tried to concentrate. How should he get there? He wasn't sure if he should make a left turn or a right turn.

If Ben turns left, go to page 39.
If Ben turns right, go to page 104.

Continued from page 38

Ben stood on the edge of the checkerboard floor. He looked up and suddenly felt very dizzy. He looked down. That felt a little safer.

"Down is always easier than up, right?" he said, trying to sound confident.

He had to try something. He took a deep breath and began to climb down the ladder.

As he climbed, all he could see beneath him was swirling white mist. He began to wonder if he had made a mistake.

Ten more steps, he thought. *And then I'll go back up.*

Ben counted the steps out loud, until he reached seven . . . eight . . . nine . . . "Ten!" Ben cried.

And he found himself on solid ground again.

The white mist parted. Ben found himself in a garden. The sky above him was bright blue. Red and blue flowers carpeted the ground.

Ben reached down to look at a flower and realized they were made of tissue paper.

They're like the fake flowers that magicians use in their acts, Ben realized. But here they seemed to be actually *growing* out of the ground.

It felt good to be off of the ladder, but Ben was

still confused. "What do I do now?" he wondered out loud.

In response to his question, one flower in the center of the garden began to grow higher and higher, stretching up on a long, green stem. The white flower bud on top of the stem was as large as Ben's head. The flower opened up, and Ben saw words written on the petals. He stepped up to get a closer look.

Picking a flower is what to do.
But should you pick red or blue?
Blue is bold, but red is rosy.
Make your choice and pick a posy.

Ben groaned. He figured out that he had to pick a flower to get out of the garden. But should he pick a red one or a blue one? The riddle wasn't very clear.

If Ben chooses the red flower, go to page 88.

If Ben chooses the blue flower, go to page 113.

Continued from page 103

Ben raised his arms and removed the silver key with his fingertips. It took a few seconds, but he managed to get the key in the lock and spring open the cuffs.

Ben pounded on the closet door. "Help!" he cried.

Ben heard footsteps in the hall and the sound of jingling keys. The door opened, and Garfield the Great stood there.

"I told you not to trust him," he said.

"He's got the magic kit," Ben said. "I've got to catch up with him. It's not too late!"

Ben ran out of the Bleaktown Home for Retired Magicians and looked up and down the street. There was no sign of Mr. Mysterioso, but Ben had an idea.

Ben turned the corner and headed toward Sebastian Cream's Curiosity Shop. Sure enough, there was Mr. Mysterioso, running down the street in his white tuxedo.

Ben picked up speed. He ran past Just Lampshades and Mel's Medical Supply.

But Sebastian Cream's Curiosity Shop was nowhere in sight. The store had disappeared!

Ahead, Mr. Mysterioso looked around him,

confused. Ben felt confused, too.

Everything was getting way too weird.

Maybe I should just go home and forget all about Dr. Presto's Magic Kit, Ben thought.

But then again, Mr. Mysterioso is *a dangerous man. He must be stopped!*

If Ben continues to chase after Mr. Mysterioso, go to page 118.

If Ben goes home, go to page 108.

Continued from page 17

"Uh, thanks, anyway," Ben told the rabbit. "But I think I'll follow the sign.

The rabbit's ears twitched. "Fine. But I warned you," it said. Then it hopped away.

Ben walked along the checkerboard floor, following the direction of the arrow. After a few steps he began to wonder if he should have followed the rabbit after all. The floor seemed to stretch out into infinity.

Just as he was about to lose hope, he came across another arrow. Ben kept walking, following the squares so that he kept on a straight path.

Then finally he made out a shape in the distance. As he walked closer, he saw that it was a tall black hat the size of a small house. Ben could make out a door in the very front of the hat.

Ben knocked on the door. "Hello! Is anyone there?" he asked.

The door slowly creaked open. A tall man stood behind it. He wore a black tuxedo. Purple silk was wrapped around his head. His thin face was sharply angled. A skinny beard formed a triangle on his chin.

"Dr. Presto!" Ben cried. Ben couldn't believe it. The great magician was standing right in front of him.

"Dr. Presto, at your service," the magician said, bowing low. He stepped aside. "Please, come in."

Ben stepped inside the hat. The small, round house was crammed with bookshelves loaded with books about magic. Silk scarves bulged from a black steamer trunk. A white dove cooed inside a golden cage. And in one corner, Ben saw a tall red cabinet painted with black dragons. The Cabinet of Doom. It was one of Dr. Presto's most famous illusions.

"What is this place?" Ben asked. "What are you doing here?"

"I should ask you the same question," Dr. Presto said. "I don't get many visitors here in Magic Limbo."

"Magic Limbo?"

"This is a magical place between worlds," the magician explained. "I discovered it in my quest to learn the secrets of magic."

"All the books say you disappeared in nineteen twenty-two," Ben said. "Have you been here all those years?"

Dr. Presto nodded. "The more famous I became, the more jealous other magicians became of my talents. They were against my rather . . . unusual methods. I came here to protect myself from their jealousy. I planned to return when it was safe."

"So why didn't you ever go back?" Ben asked.

Dr. Presto didn't answer. Instead he touched the wand in Ben's hand. "A magnificent specimen," he said. "Where did you get it?"

"It's from your magic kit!" Ben told him. "I found your kit in this weird old store. I had to buy it. You created some incredible illusions."

Dr. Presto could not take his eyes off of the wand. He stroked his beard thoughtfully. Then he snapped to attention. "Thank you, young man," he said, walking to the Cabinet of Doom. "Would you like to see one of my most famous illusions of all?"

"Of course!" Ben replied. He followed Dr. Presto to the corner. The magician opened up the cabinet. It was just as tall and just a little wider than Dr. Presto.

"The Cabinet of Doom," Dr. Presto said. "The centerpiece of my most spectacular escape illusion. Would you like to step inside?"

Ben couldn't believe his luck. First, he'd met Dr. Presto in person, and now he had the chance to actually step inside the Cabinet of Doom. It was too good to be true.

"Let me hold that for you," Dr. Presto said, pointing to the wand.

Ben handed the wand to Dr. Presto and stepped inside the cabinet.

Slam! The narrow doors slammed shut behind him.

"Hey!" Ben called out. "It's dark in here."

Dr. Presto didn't answer. Instead Ben heard him laugh maniacally. The laugh faded, and Ben heard the magician's footsteps walk out of the house.

Dr. Presto had trapped him in the Cabinet of Doom!

"Come back!" Ben screamed, but there was no reply.

He tried not to panic. There had to be some way out. He tried to remember what he had read about the cabinet.

Then it hit him: There was a secret door somewhere in the cabinet, opened by some kind of pump or lever. All Ben had to do was find it and he'd be free.

But the cabinet was so narrow that Ben could not move his arms from his sides. He searched the bottom of the cabinet with his feet.

He found two pedals. One to his left and one to his right. But which one triggered the secret door?

If Ben presses the left pedal, go to page 50.

If Ben presses the right pedal, go to page 79.

Continued from page 49

"Hurry up!" Lori wailed.

Ben decided to use the emergency spell. He wasn't 100 percent sure if reading the spell backward would bring Lori back down. Besides, something even worse could happen by reversing the spell.

Ben took a deep breath. He held the wand and read aloud the words of the emergency spell. It sounded different from the others:

"Water freeze and fire burn.
Hear my words and you'll return.
When I wave this wand of black,
Dr. Presto will come back!"

Ben waved the wand. The spell didn't seem to make any sense. What was supposed to happen?

"Ben!" Lori cried. "Look behind you!"

Ben spun around.

And found himself face-to-face with Dr. Presto!

The magician towered over Ben. He looked just like his picture. He wore the same black tuxedo. The same purple head wrap. The same thin beard. Only one thing was different: This Dr. Presto wasn't solid. He was wispy and transparent . . . just like . . .

"A ghost!" Lori shrieked.

"Dr. P-P-P-Presto," Ben sputtered. "Is that really you?"

The magician bowed. "It is I, the great Dr. Presto," he said. "Thank you for freeing me, young man."

"Freeing you?" Ben asked.

"Your lovely assistant is correct," Dr. Presto said. "I am no longer one of the living. Before I passed on, I created this magic kit as a receptacle for my spirit. Saying the spell freed my spirit from the kit."

"That's amazing!" Ben said. "You must be the greatest magician who ever lived."

"Of course," Dr. Presto replied.

"That's great," Ben went on, "because we could really use some help. I need to find out how to get Lori—I mean, my assistant—to stop levitating. Do you think you can you help us?"

Dr. Presto laughed. The room darkened as though clouds were blocking the sun. "I am not here to help *you*," he said. "You are here to help *me*."

"I-I don't like this, Ben," Lori said from above. "Do something!"

The room suddenly felt quite cold. Ben shivered. "What do you mean that I am here to help you?" he asked Dr. Presto.

"I knew that one day a magician would be intrigued by the kit and try the spells inside," Dr. Presto told Ben. "And of course I also knew that the spells would go horribly wrong, forcing the magician to use the emergency spell. Once the spell was used, I knew I'd be able to take my place among the living once more."

Uh-oh. That didn't sound good. "And, uh, how exactly are you going to do that?" Ben asked.

Dr. Presto looked right into Ben's eyes. "I will inhabit your body, of course," he said. He raised his hand and a ghostly wand appeared. "I was hoping for a more impressive vessel, but I suppose yours will have to do."

"Wait a second," Ben said, slowly backing up toward the door. "If you take over my body, then what happens to me?"

"Your spirit will be trapped in the magic kit for all eternity," Dr. Presto replied. "Just like mine was. But now, thanks to you, I'm free!" Then he let out a long, cackling laugh.

Ben's first thought was to race to the door and get as far away from Dr. Presto as he could. But then Lori would be left behind with the magician's ghost. He had to stay and stop Dr. Presto, somehow. He opened up the magic book.

"Not so fast!" The magician reached out and knocked the book out of Ben's hands. Then he raised his ghostly magic wand.

"Water burn and fire freeze.
Evil powers, hear my pleas.
When I wave this wand so fine.
This earthly body shall be mine!"

A loud thunderclap rumbled in the air as Dr. Presto waved the wand over Ben. He closed his eyes, waiting for the worst to happen.

Then there was silence.

"It didn't work!" Lori cried.

Ben opened his eyes. Dr. Presto looked furious. He glared at the ghostly wand in his hand. Then he turned to the magic kit. "My spirit wand may not work," he said. "But the real wand will!"

Dr. Presto lurched for the wand, but Ben was quicker. He grabbed the wand and held it to his chest. "Sorry," Ben said. "I can't let you have this. I've been in this body for twelve years. I'm kind of used to it."

"Such insolence!" Dr. Presto bellowed. A cold wind whipped through the room. "Give me that wand this instant!"

"Ben, break the wand!" Lori called down from the ceiling. "If you destroy the wand, he can't hurt you."

Ben looked down at the wand. "I don't know,

Lori," he said. "I need to get Skip back from wherever he is. And I need to save you. If I destroy the wand, I'll destroy the magic."

"Exactly," Lori said. "I bet if you destroy the wand you'll end all of the spells!"

"Don't listen to that silly girl!" Dr. Presto snapped. "If you destroy the wand, your friends will never be saved."

Dr. Presto could be right. If the wand held all the power, then maybe Ben should try to use it to get rid of Dr. Presto. He could try the disappearing spell he used on Skip.

If Ben listens to Lori and destroys the wand, go to page 111.

If Ben tries to use the wand to make Dr. Presto disappear, go to page 132.

Continued from page 54

"I'm sorry," Ben said, scrambling over the back of the couch. "But I really need to get out of here. Good luck with that revenge thing!"

Ben jumped to the floor. Then he ran to the ladder. He could hear the assistants right behind him.

Ben didn't look back. He climbed down the ladder and out of the room.

Finally Ben looked up. He had expected Sparky and Ruby and Clarissa to follow him, but they were nowhere in sight. The white mist swirled above him once again.

Ben looked down to find that he was climbing inside another white room. This one was small, and the walls and floor were pure white. Ben hopped off of the ladder onto the floor. "Is this the way out?" he wondered.

Then Ben noticed some writing on one of the walls. He stepped closer and saw there was a slot, like a mail slot, in one of the walls. Above it were the words INSERT WAND HERE.

Ben figured it was worth a try. There wasn't anything else to do in the room.

He started to slip the wand into the slot.

Suddenly the wand was yanked out of his

hands! The next second a white gloved hand shot out of the slot. Ben could see that it was fake. It held a small white card.

Ben took the card and read it:

Thanks for the wand!
—Dr. Presto.

"No!" Ben cried. He ran back to the ladder.

But the ladder was gone. The wall and floor were solid sheets of white. There was no way out.

"Help! Help!" Ben cried, pounding on the walls.

But there was no one to hear him scream.

THE END

Continued from page 71

Ben took a deep breath. He pressed the pedal on the right.

A small door opened on the side of the cabinet.

"I did it!" Ben shouted. "I beat the Cabinet of Doom!" Quickly Ben jumped out.

But then he remember that he was still in Magic Limbo. Getting out of this place was going to be harder than escaping from the Cabinet of Doom. There was no magic pedal to push here.

Ben knew that the only person who could help him was Dr. Presto.

Up ahead, he could see Dr. Presto's tall, dark form running in the distance. Ben sped after him.

Suddenly the checkerboard floor dead-ended into a flat white wall. Ben saw Dr. Presto stop at the wall and raise the wand. A door slowly opened up in the wall.

Dr. Presto was leaving Magic Limbo!

"Wait for me!" Ben yelled. He ran as fast as he could and slammed into Dr. Presto's back. They both went tumbling through the doorway.

Ben landed on something hard. *"Ouch!"* he said, rubbing his head. Slowly he sat up and looked around. Amazingly he was back on the front steps of his house! Lori was staring at him with her mouth wide open.

"How did you do that?" she asked. "You vanished right in front of my eyes. And then you just appeared again with that guy." She pointed to Dr. Presto, who was sprawled on Ben's front lawn.

"I am not some 'guy,'" Dr. Presto said, sounding insulted. He stood up and brushed dirt off of his tuxedo. "I am Dr. Presto, the world's greatest magician."

"No way," Lori said. She reached down and picked up the magic wand, which had fallen to the bottom step. "I guess this is yours, then."

"I'll take that," Ben said quickly, grabbing the wand. He glared at Dr. Presto. "You have a lot of explaining to do. You almost left me back in Magic Limbo!"

"*Where?*" Lori asked.

Ben and Dr. Presto ignored her. The magician smiled at Ben.

"Don't be ridiculous, young man," he said. "I knew that a fine magician such as yourself would easily escape the Cabinet of Doom. And once you mastered that, you'd be able to figure a way out of Magic Limbo. I was just giving you a challenge worthy of your talents."

Ben listened to Dr. Presto. He *thought* he sounded sincere, but Ben couldn't be sure. After all, he did lock him in the cabinet. And Ben couldn't forget what it felt like being stuck inside.

"I don't know," Ben said, still holding on to the wand. "I think you really wanted to leave me back there."

"Rubbish!" said the magician. "And to prove it to you, I will train you to become a great magician like myself. I will tell you all of my secrets."

If Ben accepts Dr. Presto's offer, go to page 41.

If Ben decides to get rid of Dr. Presto, go to page 121.

Ben decided to let the rabbit go. Someone else would take care of it. Besides, it might be big, but it was still just a rabbit. How much trouble could it cause?

Ben figured that the best thing to do would be to lie low until the whole thing blew over. He kept quiet during dinner, and his parents didn't seem to know anything about the rabbit. So far, so good. Then Ben made an excuse about having lots of homework to do, and went to bed early.

As Ben drifted off to sleep, he caught the face of Dr. Presto on the magic kit. For a second, it looked like the face was laughing at him.

It's just my imagination, Ben thought, closing his eyes. Then he drifted off to sleep.

Ooooooooweeeeeeeeee. Ooooooooooweeeeeeeeee.

A strange sound drifted in and out of Ben's dreams.

Ooooooooweeeeeeeeee. Oooooooooooweeeeeeeeee.

Ben bolted awake. The sound of sirens filled the air.

Ben's door slammed open. His mom entered the room, a look of panic on her face. "Ben, get up!" she said. "We've got to go!"

"Go where?" Ben asked, still sleepy.

His mom opened his drawers and began throwing clothes into a suitcase. "This is going to sound crazy, but a giant rabbit is terrorizing Bleaktown," she said. "It's destroyed all of the buildings downtown. It tore down all of the power lines. The police can't stop it. The fire department can't stop it. The National Guard is on its way. We've got to go, *now*."

Ben jumped out of bed, his heart pounding. "A giant rabbit, huh?" Ben asked. "Does anyone know where it came from?"

"The government is investigating," his mom replied. "I can't imagine what kind of monster could have created a rabbit like this. It's terrible."

Dr. Presto's face grinned at Ben from the magic kit. Ben quickly grabbed the kit and shoved it under his bed. "Yeah, it's pretty terrible, Mom," he said. "Just terrible."

THE END

Continued from page 60

The decision was easy. Mr. Mysterioso had said that Dr. Presto's kit was "marvelous." Garfield the Great had called it "dangerous." Obviously Garfield knew what he was talking about. That kit was definitely dangerous.

Ben turned to Garfield the Great. "If you could help me, that would be great, Mr., uh . . . Mr. Great," he said.

Garfield patted Ben on the head. "You are a smart boy. Follow me."

Garfield the Great shuffled out of the parlor. He was a tall man, and he stooped as he walked. As Ben followed him, he caught Mr. Mysterioso's eye. The magician had been scowling, but a fake smile appeared on his face when he saw Ben.

"You are making a mistake, young man," Mr. Mysterioso said. "You will find that there is nothing great about Garfield."

Garfield ignored him, and Ben did the same. He followed Garfield down a long staircase. Ben shivered. The air had suddenly become cold and damp. Was Mr. Mysterioso right? Had he made a horrible mistake?

Garfield led Ben into the basement and pulled a cord. A single lightbulb lit up the gloom, casting eerie shadows on the wall. The light illuminated an old-fashioned oil furnace in the center of the room.

Garfield opened the furnace grate to reveal orange flames leaping within. "Throw the kit into the fire," he said, "quickly!"

Ben took a step backward. He wasn't expecting this. "What about Skip?" Ben asked.

"And who is Skip?" Garfield wanted to know.

"I was trying out a trick on him, and he kind of, uh, disappeared," Ben said, feeling a bit embarrassed.

"Is that all?" Garfield said. "Did you perform any other spells?"

Ben told Garfield about the rabbit. The old magician nodded.

"Thankfully, none of this is very serious," he said. "Destroying the kit will undo all of the magic you have performed. That is why you must destroy it!"

The flames danced across Garfield's wrinkled face. He looked like some kind of ghoul.

Ben hesitated. Should he trust Garfield? Everything was happening so fast.

Garfield sighed in frustration and grabbed the kit from Ben. Then he tossed it into the flames. "There!" he said, his eyes gleaming. "At last, the evil has ended!"

That was too much for Ben. He ran up the stairs and tore out of the house. He tried not to panic. How would he save Skip now?

"Hey, Ben!" a voice called out.

Ben turned. It was Skip!

"Something weird must have happened when we tried out that trick," Skip said. "My mom just told me I was, like, missing for a day. How'd you do that?"

"It's, uh, a long story," Ben said. Garfield had been right! "Look, I gotta go."

Ben went back into the house and found Garfield. He and the old magician talked for hours.

Garfield explained that Dr. Presto was not like other illusionists. Instead of practicing magic tricks, he had searched the world to find sources of evil magic to power his tricks. When he died, it was rumored that he had preserved his spirit inside a magic kit. Garfield knew the kit was evil when he saw it.

"I can't believe I blew thirty bucks on that thing," Ben said, moaning. "Now I'll have to deliver papers for three more months to save money for the Official Junior Professional Magician's Kit."

Garfield laughed. "You don't need that, son. Why, I can teach you about magic!"

Garfield agreed to give Ben free magic lessons. Ben found that learning from a teacher was much easier than learning from a book. In no time he was performing tricks like a pro. Word got around among the magical community about Ben, and soon he was working as a professional magician.

Ben bought tickets to his first show for everyone he knew—everyone but Old Man Martin,
that is.

THE END

Ben thought about the riddle. *Blue is bold, but red is rosy.*

Hmm. Bold meant brave. But he had heard the word "rosy" in expressions before. It meant that everything would turn out good. That sounded like the best bet.

Ben reached down and picked a red flower.

He heard a scraping sound above him and looked up. A doorway slid open in the blue sky, and a golden ladder dropped down. "Cool!" Ben said. "I guess I got it right."

Ben stuck the flower in his pocket, and climbed up the ladder. He soon reached a small, white room.

The room was filled with gold cages of all shapes and sizes. Each cage was on a stand, but every stand was a different height. And in each cage was a white dove.

The doves began to make cooing noises when they saw Ben. Then one of the doves spoke up.

"Free me, Ben!" it called out. Ben looked from dove to dove until he found one moving her beak. She must have been the one talking.

"If you free me, I will lead you out of here," she said, looking Ben in the eye. "The other doves will lead you to danger."

That sounded good to Ben. He began to weave his way between the cages toward the talking dove.

Suddenly every dove in the room began to talk at once.

"Free me, Ben!"

"No, free me!"

Ben tried to stay focused on the dove that had first spoken, but it wasn't easy. Finally he reached what he thought was the right cage. This cage had a rounded top and was about a foot taller than his head.

"That's right, Ben," said the dove inside, looking down at Ben. "I will lead you to freedom."

But the dove in the cage right next to her began to flap her wings. "No, Ben. It's a trick. Open my cage, not its!"

Ben stared at the two cages. This dove was in a square cage that was just as tall as Ben. The dove stared into Ben's eyes.

"Make the right decision, Ben!" the dove pleaded.

If Ben frees the dove in the round cage, go to page 22.

If Ben frees the dove in the square cage, go to page 115.

Continued from page 107

Ben decided not to jump onto the truck. It seemed too dangerous. Instead he ran across the street before the truck passed.

The decision helped him for a few moments. The truck blocked the soldiers's view as Ben cut across the lawn of the house across the street and disappeared into the backyard.

Ben knew all of the houses from his paper route. He knew which houses were shaded by tall trees, and which yards had tall fences to keep people out. That gave him an advantage over the soldiers. He just had to keep up his speed.

Ben could hear the soldiers crashing through bushes as they tracked him. He tried to make his legs move faster. But after running from the rabbits, they felt like jelly.

Ben reached a low wooden fence separating one yard from another. He grabbed the top of the fence and tried to pull himself over.

Instead he fell back, exhausted. The fall knocked the wind out of him. When he opened his eyes, he saw the five soldiers leaning over him.

"Nice try," said one of the men. He held Ben's top hat in his hand. Another soldier held the wand.

They must have fallen when I fell. That's what happened! Ben realized.

Ben could still feel the magic book in his back pocket. The soldiers must not have noticed it. That was just fine with him. It might come in handy.

The soldiers dragged Ben out to the street. A black Jeep pulled up. Two of the men pushed Ben into the backseat and surrounded him on either side.

"Help!" Ben yelled. But the roaring motor of the Jeep drowned out his voice.

"Where are we going?" Ben asked the men.

"You'll know soon enough," one of the soldiers said mysteriously.

Ben settled back in his seat. He thought about jumping out of the Jeep, but it was moving too fast. The soldiers had said that someone was interested in his magic kit. He guessed he'd soon find out who it was.

They rode through Bleaktown to the edge of town until they reached a gray concrete building. A large door, at the side of the building, opened up, and the Jeep drove inside.

Ben saw they were in a large room filled with strange machines that seemed to be made of plastic tubes and blinking lights. A man in a white lab coat was fiddling with one of the machines. Gray hair stuck straight up from the top of his head. He smiled when he saw the Jeep pull up.

"Good work, men," the strange man said. He took the hat and wand from the soldiers. "Excellent."

"Who are you?" Ben asked, climbing out of the Jeep. "What do you want?"

"Why, the secrets of magic, of course!" he replied, staring at the hat and wand in wonder. Then he turned to Ben. "Allow me to introduce myself," he said. "I am Maximillian Fuller, scientist. Welcome to my secret laboratory."

Go to page 25.

Continued from page 99

"We're going to be famous," Lori said, her eyes shining.

Ben's feeling of guilt vanished as he imagined himself on stage again, in front of thousands of adoring fans. He could just hear the crowds cheering! So what if his tricks were the result of a special magic kit? Some people were born with amazing singing voices. Did it really matter where his talent came from?

"We will be famous," Ben promised. "Because I am going to do a trick on the television show that no one will forget!"

Ben knew just what he wanted to do. He'd perform an incredible escape. This would win the contest for sure.

Ben spent all week planning out the trick. First he'd have Lori tie his hands behind his back. Then he'd step inside a cabinet on the stage. Lori would get the audience to count to three, and when she opened the cabinet, Ben would be gone. The audience would gasp with amazement to find him floating above their heads.

It was complicated. Ben would have to use several of Dr. Presto's spells in a row. But he was sure he could do it. He just had to say a bunch of words and wave the wand, right?

The day of the show came before Ben knew it. Ben and Lori waited backstage. The show had provided the cabinet for Ben. They were all set. Then Ben heard his name being announced from on stage.

"Presenting the Amazing Ben and his lovely assistant, Lori!"

Ben and Lori stepped out. He talked to the crowd as Lori tied his hands with the rope. They had practiced so that Lori would tie a loose knot. Ben would slip out of the knot and take the wand from his pocket to cast the spells.

Ben stepped into the cabinet, and Lori shut the door. He didn't have much time. He quickly freed his hands and grabbed the wand.

Then his mind went blank.

His palms began to sweat. What spell was he supposed to do now? The levitation? No, the vanishing spell. Or maybe the transportation spell. But how did it go?

Outside the cabinet, he heard Lori cry, "One, two, three!"

The cabinet doors open. Ben looked out at the crowd and gave a sheepish wave. "Uh, can we start over?"

The crowd booed loudly.

The host of the show came back out on stage.

"Let's hear it for the worst act ever in the history of our show!"

"So much for being famous," Ben said, groaning.

"We are famous," Lori said. "Famously awful!"

THE END

Continued from pages 117 and 122

Ben decided to try out for the talent show. After all, he reasoned, did it really matter if his tricks succeeded because of some wires and gimmicks, or because of real magic? No one would ever have to find out.

All week, Ben and Lori looked through the book for the best tricks. Lori agreed to be Ben's assistant.

They decided to start small, with tricks that would be easy and pretty safe.

Pulling a rabbit out of a hat was a good one, of course. Then Ben found a spell that could transform silk scarves into a flock of doves.

For their final trick, they decided to levitate Lori—make her float in air. Before Lori would agree to practice it, they made sure to find a spell that could bring Lori back to the ground. Ben practiced levitating apples and oranges first to make sure he got things right.

Finally the day of the tryouts came. Ben and Lori lined up outside the Bleaktown Theater early in the morning. It looked like they had a long wait ahead. Everyone on line was practicing some kind of skill or trick—juggling, singing scales, or twirling around in dance shoes. Ben felt a little guilty watching everyone on line work so hard. It almost felt like cheating to use Dr. Presto's kit.

But it was too late to back out now. He and Lori had tried to get dressed up for the occasion, but Ben wasn't sure if they looked magical enough. Ben didn't have a tuxedo, so he had settled on a black T-shirt and jeans. He had borrowed a red tie from his dad and tied it around his head like a headband. Ben thought it made him look mysterious.

Lori didn't own any fancy gowns. In fact there wasn't a single skirt or dress in her closet. But she wore her cleanest pair of jeans. She had even picked a flower from her garden and stuck it behind her ear.

It seemed like hours before Ben and Lori were called inside. Finally a young woman with spiky hair and glasses stuck her head out of the stage door. "Next!" she shouted.

Ben and Lori followed her inside. She led them into a small theater. Two women and one man sat in the front row. They were all scribbling in notebooks.

The girl with the glasses asked Ben and Lori for their names. Then she led them up on stage. As Ben looked out into the theater, he felt nervous. Standing up there was way different from doing magic tricks on his front steps.

One of the women had red hair piled on top of her head. She leaned forward in her seat. "We'll be judging your act," she said. "If you impress us, you'll be flown to California next week to compete on television."

Ben and Lori nodded.

"What are you going to do today?" the woman asked.

Ben started to answer, but a sound like a frog croak came out. He cleared his throat. "It's a magic act."

The judges snickered.

"Make it quick," the woman said, rolling her eyes.

Ben took a deep breath and began. He pulled a rabbit out of a hat. The judges sat up a little straighter.

Then Ben tossed five scarves in the air. The judges watched in amazement as they transformed into five beautiful white doves. Ben ended the performance by making Lori levitate. She even did a few fancy somersaults in midair to show off. The flower fell out of her hair, but the judges didn't seem to care.

"Fabulous!" said the redhead. "You two are going to California!"

"*Yes!*" Ben shouted, giving Lori a high five. He

packed the magic kit and walked backstage. Ben did a quick disappearing spell to take care of the rabbit and the doves.

"We did it, Ben!" Lori said, excitedly.

But Ben didn't look so happy anymore.

"What's the matter?" Lori asked. "A minute ago you were psyched. Now you look like you just failed the biggest test of the year.

Ben shrugged. "I'm not so sure about this anymore," he said.

"You're not so sure about *what*?" Lori wanted to know.

"I mean, I don't feel so great about using Dr. Presto's magic to win the contest," Ben explained. "Maybe we should just forget about the kit and stick with the kinds of tricks I used to do."

If Ben uses Dr. Presto's magic in the talent contest, go to page 93.

If Ben uses his regular magic tricks in the talent contest, go to page 134.

Continued from page 60

Something about Mr. Mysterioso's bright white suit and even brighter smile were hypnotizing to Ben. It couldn't hurt to at least talk to the old guy, could it?

"Uh, I'll see you later, Mr. . . . Mr. Great," Ben told Garfield the Great. "Thanks, anyway, though."

"Excellent, young man," Mr. Mysterioso said, putting an arm around Ben. "Let us go into my office and take a look at that magic kit of yours."

Ben followed Mr. Mysterioso out of the parlor and down a dim hallway. The magician opened a door and stepped into an incredibly small room. So small, in fact, that Ben was pretty sure it was a closet.

Every inch of wall space was covered with pictures of Mr. Mysterioso doing his magic act. Most were in black-and-white. A tall shelf on the back wall held all kinds of props for magical tricks. The only other furniture in the room were two folding chairs.

Mr. Mysterioso sat down and motioned for Ben to do the same. He looked at the magic kit with greedy eyes.

"So, young man . . ."

"Ben," Ben said.

Mr. Mysterioso nodded. "Ben. How did this fine magic kit fall into your hands?"

Ben told the magician about Sebastian Cream's Curiosity Shop.

"I see," Mr. Mysterioso replied. "And why did you bring it here to our humble residence?"

"It's because of Skip," Ben said. "My mailman. I followed the directions in the kit to make Skip disappear. And he did."

Mysterioso chuckled. "Isn't that what was supposed to happen?"

Ben shook his head. "No, I mean he *really* disappeared. He's gone. Vanished. His mom told the police he's been missing all night."

The magician's eyes gleamed. "I see," he said. "I have heard that Dr. Presto's magic kit was . . . extraordinary. If what you are saying is true, then the rumors must be correct. I must examine the kit." He held out his hands. His smile had turned into a sinister grimace.

Ben held on tightly to the kit. "I need you to help me get Skip back," Ben said. "Then you can do whatever you want with it."

"Of course," Mr. Mysterioso said, his smile returning. "We will help Skip. But, of course, I must see the kit first."

Ben reluctantly handed the kit over to the magician. "I followed the instructions in the book," Ben said. "But it's hard to make sense out of most of the spells. They're like in some weird language or something."

Mr. Mysterioso slowly turned the pages of the book. "Aha!" he cried out. "I see something here that will help us."

"What is it?" Ben asked, trying to see the pages, but Mr. Mysterioso stood up quickly.

"It says, 'To undo the spell cast by a magician, the magician's hands must be bound. Then another magician can undo the spell.'"

"Bind my hands?" Ben said. "You mean, like, with rope?"

Mr. Mysterioso reached over to the shelf and pulled off a pair of handcuffs. "How about these?" he asked. "No magician is without a pair of magic handcuffs. They should do the trick."

Ben shrugged. He was anxious to help Skip. If all it took was wearing some handcuffs for a while, he'd do it.

Mr. Mysterioso clamped the cuffs down tightly onto Ben's wrists. Then he picked up Dr. Presto's kit.

"Can you reverse the spell on Skip now?" Ben asked.

"Of course I *can*," Mr. Mysterioso said. "But I

won't!"

Before Ben could react, Mysterioso darted out of the office, slamming the closet door behind him. Ben ran to the door and tried the handle with his fingertips. It was locked tightly.

Ben tried to calm his thoughts. Harry Houdini had become famous by escaping from all kinds of handcuffs. Ben struggled to remember how he did it.

Houdini sometimes had a key hidden on him, Ben remembered. A master key that could open almost any pair of handcuffs. But that didn't do Ben any good. He didn't have a key hidden on him.

But maybe Mr. Mysterioso did. Ben turned around in the closet, searching for any sign of a key. With surprise he realized two were in plain sight. One gold key and one silver key hung on hooks next to the door.

Ben knew he didn't have much time to catch Mr. Mysterioso. He had to act fast. He had to act *now*.

All Ben had to do was pick the right key.

If Ben chooses the gold key, go to page 123.

If Ben chooses the silver key, go to page 66.

Continued from page 63

Ben had no time to think. When he reached the end of Maple Street he turned to the right. In the distance, he could see the large archway that marked the entrance to the gardens. If he hadn't been running so fast, he would have breathed a sigh of relief.

The rabbits got closer and closer with each hop. Ben's heart pounded furiously as he ran toward the gardens. The rubber soles of his sneakers burned as they slapped the hard pavement.

Ben shot through the archway and ran through the gardens until he couldn't run any farther. Then he stopped and doubled over, puffing and panting. He didn't care if the rabbits got him now. He had nothing left in him.

Then Ben realized that the thundering sound of giant rabbit feet had stopped. He straightened up to see the rabbits scattered around the garden, munching on every green thing in sight.

His plan had worked! Perfect! Now he just had to find some way to get rid of them.

Ben took the book out of his pocket. He thought about trying the shrinking spell, but knew he'd never be able to tap all five rabbits with the wand. He turned the page and found an enlarging spell. Ben groaned.

Just what I need, he thought. *Bigger rabbits.*

Ben took off the top hat and wiped some sweat from his forehead. He started to put the hat back on, then stopped. He had an idea.

"It's worth a try," Ben said out loud. He put the hat on the ground in front of him.

Ben held the wand over the hat. Then he read the words from the enlarging spell: "Gigantus titanus!"

Ben tapped the hat with the wand.

Then he ran.

The ground trembled. Before his eyes the hat grew to the size of a small house. "Awesome," Ben said.

Each of the giant rabbits stopped munching and turned toward the hat, transfixed. They slowly hopped across the grass toward the hat.

Ben grinned. It's just what he had hoped. No magic rabbit could resist a magic hat. It was in their nature.

One by one, the rabbits jumped into the hat. When the last fluffy tail had disappeared over the brim, Ben rushed to the hat and read the shrinking spell. Then he tapped the hat with the wand.

With a poof of smoke, the hat transformed back into its normal size. Ben picked it up and looked inside.

The rabbits were gone. Completely gone.

"I did it!" Ben shouted. He stared at the wand in his hand. Dr. Presto's Magic Kit was the most incredible thing he had ever seen. Now that he had the rabbit situation under control, there was no telling what amazing things he could do.

First thing's first. Lori was back home with a hurt ankle. Ben had to go tell her that everything was all right. He stuffed the book back into his pocket and put the hat back on his head.

"Stop right there!"

Ben froze in position. A group of men ran up from behind and formed a circle around him. They looked like soldiers, but not the army guys you see on TV. They wore black turtleneck shirts, black pants, and black boots. Each soldier had a strange-looking weapon slung over his shoulder.

One of the soldiers stepped forward. "You need to come with us," he barked. "Someone is very interested in this magic kit of yours."

Ben didn't like the sound of that. He had outran a gang of giant rabbits. A few creepy soldiers shouldn't be a problem. "Hey!" Ben yelled. "There's a giant rabbit behind you!"

Every soldier turned to look. It was all Ben

needed. He broke through the circle and ran through the gardens as fast as he could.

The soldiers yelled and scrambled after him. Ben reached the back gate and ran through it. Ben looked down the street. He knew the neighborhood pretty well. He could run through the houses and maybe lose the soldiers.

Then a garbage truck turned the corner. Ben eyed the ladder on the back of the truck. If he grabbed on, he'd get a free ride. Maybe that was his best bet.

If Ben hitches a ride on the garbage truck, go to page 44.

If Ben decides to keep running, go to page 90.

Continued from page 67

Ben turned away and walked home. It was all too much. A rabbit appearing out of nowhere. A mailman—and a store—vanishing into thin air. An evil magician trapping him in a closet. Ben let out a big sigh. He couldn't handle any more magic.

I'm going to go home, Ben thought, *I'm going to straight into my room, turn on the TV, and never do another magic trick again.*

But when Ben neared his house his saw two police cruisers parked in front. Four uniformed officers stood on his front steps. What could possibly be going on? He ran up to his front door.

"Ben Michaels?" one of the officers asked.

Ben nodded.

"You are wanted for questioning in the disappearance of mail carrier Skip Feeney," the officer told him. "Eyewitnesses say that this was the last house Skip visited before he disappeared."

"I can explain," Ben blurted out. "You see, I have this magic kit. I made Skip disappear. He vanished into thin air."

Ben stopped talking. He didn't know what esle to say. The officers had to believe him, right?

The police officers exchanged glances. "Looks like we got a loony here," one of them said, snapping the cuffs on Ben.

"But it really happened!" Ben wailed.

"That's enough, son," said the officer. "You have the right to remain silent!"

THE END

Continued from page 117

"I think I'll pass on that talent show," Ben said.

Lori frowned. "Okay. But that doesn't mean we can't have fun with the kit. We should look through the book again. Maybe you can make money appear out of thin air or something."

Ben thought about what he had gone through in Magic Limbo. It definitely *wasn't* fun. It worried him to think what other horrors the magic kit might have in store for him. "I don't think it's such a good idea," he told Lori. "In fact, there's only one thing I want to do with this kit."

"What's that?" Lori asked.

"Take it back where I got it," Ben replied. "To Sebastian Cream's Curiosity Shop."

Go to page 137.

Continued from page 76

"Give me the wand, Ben," Dr. Presto said, slowly floating closer. "It's the only way to save your friends."

Who was Ben going to trust: an evil ghost, or his best friend? It was an easy choice.

Ben snapped the wand into two pieces. "So long, Dr. Presto!" he cried.

"Noooooo!" Dr. Presto wailed. His ghostly body separated into millions of glowing particles. The particles swirled in circles, and then suddenly exploded.

Dr. Presto was gone.

"Whoa!" Lori fell from the ceiling and landed on Ben's bed with a thud.

"Are you okay?" Ben asked, running to her side.

"Yeah," Lori replied. "That was definitely weird."

"You can say that again," Ben said. "Hey, I wonder if this means that Skip is all right!"

Ben and Lori ran down the stairs and out Ben's front door. There, standing in front of the tree in Ben's lawn, was Skip.

"Did the trick work?" Skip asked. He looked groggy and confused.

Ben and Lori looked at each other.

"It worked better than we expected," Ben finally said. "You, uh, should probably go home to your mom now. I think she's worried about you."

Skip looked at his full mailbag. "But what about my letters?" he asked, still dazed.

"Don't worry about them right now," Lori said. "You really should go home."

"Okay," Skip said. He scratched his head, hoisted his bag onto his shoulders, and walked down the street.

"So I guess I was wrong about the kit," Lori told Ben. "It really was magic."

"Maybe," Ben said. "But I wasn't expecting it to be haunted by an evil ghost. I'm taking the kit back to Sebastian Cream's Curiosity Shop before anything else happens!"

Go to page 137.

Ben stared at the riddle again. *Blue is bold, but red is rosy.*

Well, bold meant brave. And being brave was a good thing, right? He reached down and picked a blue flower.

As soon as he plucked the stem, a strange, sweet scent filled the air. Ben coughed as the smell entered his nostrils, almost knocking him off of his feet.

And then he suddenly felt sleepy. His eyes closed, and he felt himself sinking down into the garden of flowers.

When he finally woke up, Ben felt groggy. He opened his eyes, expecting to see the blue sky above.

Instead he saw a ceiling. *His* ceiling.

Ben bolted upright. He was back home, in his bed. He was even wearing his pajamas.

"It was all a dream," Ben said, relieved. "That explains everything."

Ben got out of bed. Something wasn't quite right, he knew. The room was dusty, and the air felt stale. The posters on his walls were yellow and frayed.

Ben shrugged. After his Magic Limbo dream,

nothing much was going to worry him.

Ben got up and walked downstairs. It was time for breakfast.

But there was no one home. The furniture was covered with dust. The downstairs windows had been boarded up.

A strange feeling crept over Ben. Something was definitely not right.

Ben stepped outside. The minivan in Lori's driveway was gone. In its place was a strange-looking silver car.

Ben spotted a newspaper on Lori's front lawn. He ran over, picked it up, and looked at the date.

"This can't be right," Ben said, gasping, and dropping the paper. "That date is fifty years in the future."

He must have picked the wrong flower!

"Noooooooooo!" Ben screamed.

THE END

Continued from page 89

Ben closed his eyes. He tried to picture what the dove had looked like when it first spoke to him. He remembered that the dove had looked him right in the eyes.

Of course! The dove in the round cage was too high to look him directly in the eye. The dove in the square cage must be the right one.

Ben opened the door to the gold cage.

The dove flew out and landed on Ben's shoulder. "You made the right choice," she said. "The other doves here are evil magicians who have been transformed. If you had freed one of them, he would have switched places with you."

Ben shuddered. The thought of being turned into a dove and trapped in a cage was just too creepy. "Let's get out of here," he said.

"Follow me," the dove said, flying off of his shoulder.

Ben followed the dove as she wove between the cages. She stopped in front of one of the plain white walls.

"Just touch the wall with the wand, close your eyes, and pass through here," she said. "It will take you home."

"Thanks!" Ben said. "Can't you come, too?"

"I must stay here to protect others like you," she said. "Now go. Quickly!"

"Right," Ben replied. He looked at the wall. It seemed perfectly solid to him.

"Trust me!" the dove called out.

Ben tapped the wand to the wall. He closed his eyes. He took a step forward . . .

"That was incredible!"

Ben opened his eyes. He was back on his front steps. Lori was standing next to him with an amazed expression on her face. "Ben, you did it! You actually did it!" Lori cried.

Ben felt a little strange, and very confused. He wasn't sure exactly *what* he had done. "So, what did you see, exactly?" he asked Lori.

"It was so cool," Lori said excitedly. "You said the spell. Then you tapped your head with the wand. There was a puff of smoke, and you vanished! Completely! Right before my eyes."

"And then what?" Ben asked.

"A few seconds later, you appeared again, like out of nowhere," she said.

A few seconds later. That was weird. Ben had been in Magic Limbo for at least a half hour.

"So, come on, Ben," Lori pleaded. "You have to tell me how you did it. I'm your best friend."

"You won't believe me," Ben said.

"Try me!"

So Ben told Lori all about his adventures in Magic Limbo. She listened, spellbound, until he was finished. "Awesome," she said. "This kit really *is* magic after all."

Ben picked up the kit. "I guess so," he said. "So what do I do now?"

"I know just the thing," Lori said. She took a newspaper clipping out of her jeans pocket. "There are talent scouts for a TV show coming to Bleaktown next week. They're looking for all kinds of acts. I think you should try out."

Ben looked at the article. It certainly was tempting. The winner of the show would get to compete with talent from all around the country. He'd be famous.

Just like Harry Houdini.

But then he realized that wasn't exactly true. Harry Houdini had been a skilled illusionist. He had performed his tricks with magic, not with skill. If Ben used the kit to win the contest, it would be like cheating.

If Ben goes on the talent show, go to page 96.

If Ben decides he has had enough of magic, go to page 110.

117

Continued from page 67

Ben sighed. He had started this thing. Now he had to finish it. "Mr. Mysterioso!" Ben yelled.

Mr. Mysterioso turned around. He looked surprised to see Ben. "Wh-What are you doing here?" he asked.

"I surprised you, huh?" Ben said. "I escaped your little trap. When you stole the magic kit, you didn't steal *all* of Dr. Presto's magic. I still have something you need." It was a lie, of course, but Ben was counting on it to work.

Mysterioso carefully stepped toward Ben. "Is that so?" he said.

"That's right," Ben said. "I have a piece of the kit that you need. And I'll give it to you—but you've got to first bring Skip back."

Mr. Mysterioso thought about what Ben had said. Ben held his breath and crossed his fingers, hoping this would work.

"Fine," Mr. Mysterioso finally agreed. "You can have your precious mailman. But give me the piece first."

Ben shook his head. "No way. Not until I see Skip."

Mr. Mysterioso frowned, but he didn't change his mind about bringing Skip back. He raised the wand in the air. "Reapparensis, visibilus!" he cried.

Poof! Skip appeared in front of them in a puff of smoke. He looked dazed. "What happened?" he asked.

"I'll tell you later," Ben whispered quickly. "First, I need you to tackle that guy. He stole my magic kit!"

Skip looked at Ben. Then he looked at Mr. Mysterioso. The magician started to run.

"Okay!" Skip said, racing after Mr. Mysterioso. With just a few short steps, Skip caught up with the magician. Skip wrapped his arms around Mr. Mysterioso and threw him to the ground.

"This is an outrage!" Mr. Mysterioso cried.

"Get the magic kit!" Ben cried, running up to them.

Skip wrestled the kit out of his hands and handed it to Ben. "What now?" he asked.

"Let's go to your house," Ben suggested. "I think your mom is worried about you."

Mr. Mysterioso's screams faded as they walked down the street. Ben told Skip everything that had happened after he'd performed the trick. Skip didn't remember a thing about his disappearance. He had a hard time believing he had been missing for a whole day.

"What are you going to do with that magic kit

now?" Skip asked.

"I think I know someone who can keep it safe," Ben said, thinking of Garfield the Great.

"What, no more magic?" Skip asked.

Ben thought about it. He'd had about as much magic as he could handle. "I think I'm going to save my money for a bike," Ben said.

THE END

Studying under Dr. Presto would bring Ben fame and fortune. But he just couldn't bring himself to trust the magician.

He wasn't sure what to do next. Who knew what other sinister tricks Dr. Presto held up his sleeve?

"Magic lessons sounds great," Ben lied. He began to climb up his front steps one at a time. "I just have to, uh, ask my mother first. I'll be right out."

Anger flashed across Dr. Presto's face. "Give me my wand!" he bellowed.

Ben scooped up the magic kit in one hand. He grabbed Lori's hand with the other. "Come on!" he yelled, dragging her inside the house.

Ben locked the door behind him. Then he ran to the front window and looked outside. Dr. Presto stood in front of the glass, shaking his fist. "You can't stay in there forever!" he yelled.

"Quick, Lori," Ben said. "Look through the book. Find that disappearing spell again."

Lori flipped through the pages. "Here it is," she said, thrusting the book under Ben's face.

Ben looked at the words. Then he opened the window. He leaned out and held the wand over

Dr. Presto's head. "Here it is," Ben taunted. "Come and get it!"

Dr. Presto jumped up.

"Exvanire, disapparensis, departire!" Ben cried.

Poof! A cloud of smoke appeared. When it cleared, Dr. Presto was gone.

Ben closed the window and sank into his couch. He couldn't believe everything that had happened today. Had it all been real?

"Ben, this is truly amazing," Lori said. "You could be famous with this kit. There's a TV talent show coming to town. You should go on with your magic act. The winner of the show gets to compete against talent from all around the country."

"Let me think about it," Ben said. "Right now, I'm just a little tired of magic!"

Go to page 96.

Continued from page 103

Ben lifted his arms and used his fingertips to lift the gold key off of the hook.

A groaning sound caused him to jump back, startled.

A wall of metal bars slammed down in front of the door, nearly missing Ben. The sound of footsteps clattered down the hallway as the magicians ran—as fast as impossibly old men can run—to the closet.

"Get the key! The key!" someone cried.

A few seconds later, the door opened. The magicians stared through the metal bars at Ben.

"I picked the wrong key," Ben said weakly.

Garfield the Great shook his head. "You should have listened to me," he said. "Where is Mr. Mysterioso?"

"He took Dr. Presto's kit and ran off," Ben said.

"Then we are all doomed," Garfield said, sighing. "We might as well get you out. Use the silver key to unlock your handcuffs."

While Ben struggled with the cuffs, some of the magicians sawed at the bars with hacksaws. Ben sat back, bored and embarrassed, as the men worked.

Two hours later, there was a hole big enough for Ben to crawl through. "I'm sorry," he told Garfield. "But things can't be that bad, can it? I mean, what can Mr. Mysterioso do?"

"He's on TV! He's on TV!" cried a voice from the parlor.

Garfield and Ben ran to the parlor. There, on the television, was Mr. Mysterioso. He glared at the cameras, pointing his wand straight at them. "From this moment on, I am your new ruler!" Mr. Mysterioso cried. "You will all bow before me!"

Garfield looked at Ben. "I guess I made the wrong choice!" Ben admitted.

THE END

Continued from page 54

Ben was about to turn and run back down the ladder, but he caught Sparky's eye. He looked sad and tired, not dangerous. Ben tried to imagine what it was like for them to be trapped in Magic Limbo for so long. It must have been awful.

"What kind of revenge did you guys have in mind?" Ben asked. "I mean, I don't want to hurt anybody."

"The best revenge would be to make sure that Dr. Presto stays in Magic Limbo forever," Ruby said. "But as long as his magic kit exists, there's a chance he'll escape into the real world again. Then he'll send more people here."

"You mean Dr. Presto is *here*?" Ben asked.

Sparky nodded. "The other magicians found out that Dr. Presto was using evil magic to create his illusions. They wanted to ban him from performing magic. Dr. Presto sent himself here so he could lie low and come back when his rivals had all passed on. But he made one mistake: He left the wand back in the real world."

"He must know that you are here with the wand," Clarissa said. "He knows everything. And when he finds you, he will take the wand and leave you here forever."

125

"Then we need to get back to my world right now," Ben said. "Once we're there, we can destroy the wand and the magic kit. That way Dr. Presto will never be able to come back."

The assistants agreed it was a good idea. They led Ben to a tall bookcase stacked against the wall.

"Tap your wand on the bookcase three times," Ruby said.

Ben did as Ruby said.

Tap. Tap. Tap.

The bookcase creaked open, revealing a narrow staircase. At the top Ben could make out a red door.

"You lead the way," Sparky told him.

The steps groaned as Ben climbed each one. He was about to land on the final step when a cloud of smoke exploded in front of him.

Ben coughed and waved the smoke away. The smoke cleared to reveal a tall man standing in front of a red door. He wore a black tuxedo and a wrap of purple silk on his head. He had a sharp, thin face, and a slim black beard.

"Dr. Presto!" Ben and the others cried at once.

Dr. Presto's dark eyes were fixed on Ben. "I think you have something that belongs to me," he said, holding out his hand. Ben instinctively held the wand behind his back.

"Don't give it to him!" Sparky called out.

"Use it against him," Ruby cried. "Make him disappear."

Ben struggled to remember the words he had used to make himself vanish. They sounded like Latin.

Ben took a step back and held up the wand. "Uh, ex . . . ex . . . excellent . . ." Ben couldn't remember them.

"Exvanire!" Sparky cried.

"Disapparensis!" Ruby shouted.

"Departire!" Clarissa called out.

"Right!" Ben said. "Exvanire, disapparensis, departire!"

"Noooo!" Dr. Presto shrieked. Another cloud of smoke appeared, and Dr. Presto was gone.

"Where is he?" Ben asked.

"Probably sent to another part of Magic Limbo," Ruby said. "He'll be back. Hurry!"

Ben ran to the red door and tapped it with the wand three times. The door opened, and Ben stepped out of the staircase. The others followed.

To Ben's amazement he found himself back on his front steps. Lori was staring at them all with a look of frozen amazement on her face. "Who are these guys?" she said finally.

Ben explained the whole story. Lori agreed that destroying the magic kit was the best thing to do, and they threw it in her family's fireplace.

Then Ben and Lori found themselves staring at Sparky, Ruby, and Clarissa.

"What now?" Ben asked.

"I'm not sure," Ruby said. "Dr. Presto sent us all to Magic Limbo in the early nineteen hundreds. No one we know is alive anymore."

"We're good magician's assistants, though," Sparky said. "Maybe there are some magicians who could use us."

Ben had an idea. He went home and got the latest copy of *Junior Magicians' Monthly*. He called the magazine editors, and they were happy to find jobs for the assistants. So happy, in fact, that they gave Ben an Official Junior Professional Magician's Kit for free.

"Thanks, kid," Ruby said, as the assistants left for their new jobs. "We owe you one."

Ben grinned. "When I become a world-famous magician, you guys can come work for me!"

THE END

Continued from page 35

"Let's try the shrinking spell," Ben decided. "At least we know for sure what it does."

Ben took the book from Lori and turned the pages until he found the spell. It seemed simple enough.

To make something shrink:
Say these words: Smallus minutus!
Then tap the object with the wand.

The only hard thing would be tapping the rabbit with the wand. Ben took the remote and carefully hit the UP button, raising the garage door just a few inches off of the ground. Then he quickly stopped it.

Inside the garage, the rabbit let out an angry squeal. It slammed its fluffy tail against the garage door.

"That is not a happy bunny," Lori said, taking a few steps away from the garage door.

"No kidding," Ben replied. "I'd better do this quick. I don't want that rabbit crashing through the garage door."

Ben held the wand out in front of him. "Smallus minutus!" he cried. Then he leaned toward the garage. Some of the rabbit's white fur was visible under the crack at the bottom of the door. All he had to do was touch it with the wand. . . .

Slam! The rabbit kicked back with all its might.

The wand flew out of Ben's hands. It grazed his shoulder as it whizzed past him. Lori leaped forward and caught it. "Better try again," Lori said.

But Ben suddenly felt strange. His whole body began to tingle.

He looked at Lori. She had a strange look on her face. Something weird was definitely going on here.

And then their bodies began to change. Ben watched, terrified, as Lori's body began to shrink before his eyes.

With horror, he realized he was shrinking too.

"It's the wand!" Ben yelled, but his voice sounded high and squeaky. "It touched us both!"

The tingling stopped. Ben tried to get his bearings. The garage towered above them like a tall skyscraper.

"The wand is down there!" Lori said, pointing to something that looked like a tree trunk lying in the driveway. "Let's get it and change ourselves back!"

But a loud crash made Ben turn around. The rabbit had burst through the garage door. The ground shook as it backed out of the garage.

"Run!" Ben cried. He and Lori tore out of the driveway and landed on a patch of soft grass.

The rabbit turned around and stomped down the driveway. Ben and Lori ran after it.

And then they saw the wand. The giant rabbit had smashed it to pieces.

"Oh, no!" Ben wailed. "Now we'll be small forever!"

THE END

Continued from page 76

Ben made up his mind. The wand had power. And he could use that power to get rid of Dr. Presto.

The magician stared at Ben, waiting to see what he would do. Ben searched his mind, trying to remember the spell he had used on Skip. There were words: *exvanire, disapparensis, departire.* And there was something with the wand.

He had held it above Skip's head. That was it.

Ben raised the wand and ran at Dr. Presto.

"Ben, no!" Lori screamed.

Dr. Presto smacked the wand out of Ben's hand. It landed across the room.

Ben dove for the wand, but Dr. Presto flew right past him. He grabbed the wand and then straightened up, once again towering over Ben. An evil grin spread across his face. He held up the wand. "Prepare to meet your fate," he said.

"Ben, run!" Lori yelled.

But Ben couldn't do it. He couldn't leave Lori behind.

Dr. Presto recited the spell once again.

"Water burn and fire freeze.
Evil powers, hear my pleas.

When I wave this wand so fine
This earthly body shall be mine!"

Ben's head suddenly felt light. Then everything went black.

Seconds later, Ben felt like he was waking up from a sleep. He was still in his room. Lori was still clinging to the ceiling fan.

"Hey!" he said. "The spell didn't work!"

"Yes, it did," said a voice.

Ben tried to turn his head, but realized he couldn't. A figure came forward and stood in front of him.

It was his own body!

"Thank you for freeing me," Dr. Presto said, controlling Ben's body now. "And now I must leave this place and begin my quest to rule the world!"

"No! Come back!" Ben screamed as he watched Dr. Presto—in his body—leave the room. Then he looked up at Lori. "Lori," he said slowly. "If Dr. Presto is in my body, then where am I?"

Lori stared at Ben with a look of horror on her face. "Your face is on the magic kit, Ben," she said, "where Dr. Presto's used to be. He's trapped you inside the kit forever!"

"Noooooooooooo!" Ben screamed.

THE END

Continued from page 99

It just didn't feel right. Ben would always know that he was famous because of the strange powers in Dr. Presto's kit—not because he was a truly great magician like Houdini. He wasn't sure if he could live with that.

"We've got some practicing to do before we go to California, Lori," Ben said. "But we're not going to use Dr. Presto's kit."

Lori stopped short. "We're *not*? But what will we do?"

Ben smiled. "Some good old-fashioned magic. Like the kind I used to do before I had this crazy kit."

Lori agreed with Ben.

They had another week before the trip to California, and Ben and Lori practiced during every spare minute. Their parents were so proud that their children were going to be on TV. Ben didn't want to let anybody down.

Before they left, Ben tucked the magic kit safely under his bed. The face of Dr. Presto seemed to glare at him from the lid.

"I'll show you, Dr. Presto," Ben announced. "You don't need strange powers to be a great magician."

On the night of the show, Ben felt more nervous than ever. The television show's producers had costumes made for Ben and Lori. Ben wore a tuxedo covered with black sequins. Lori had on a pink sequined dress with fluffy feathers on the bottom of the skirt.

After what seemed like forever, the announcer called Ben's name. Ben and Lori stepped out onto the stage. Bright lights nearly blinded him, but Ben soon got used to them. Then Ben began his act.

Ben did all of his best tricks. He made a quarter appear out of thin air. He cut a rope in half and then made it whole again. He made a drinking glass pass right through a solid table. Ben had practiced the tricks for years and knew them really well. There was nothing magic about them—just a few props and a lot of practice. He and Lori joked around the whole time, entertaining the crowd.

The crowd really seemed to like the show. As Ben and Lori left the stage, the audience cheered. Then it was time to announce the winner. All of the acts came out on stage.

The host stepped up to the microphone. "And the winner is"—Ben gave Lori a hopeful look—"Jared the Fire-eating Tuba Player!"

Ben was disappointed, but he didn't feel as bad

as he thought he would. He had done a good job, and that was all that mattered.

Backstage, the host gave Ben a pat on the back. "Keep it up, kid," he said. "You were great. You could be a real Houdini one day."

Ben smiled. The host was right.

And he was just getting started.

THE END

Continued from pages 19, 45, 110, 112

The bell over the door tinkled as Ben walked into Sebastian Cream's Curiosity Shop. The old man was sitting behind the counter, scribbling something into a brown leather book. He did not seem to notice Ben.

Ben cleared his throat. Then he put the magic kit on the counter. "I'd like to return this, please," he said.

Mr. Cream looked up from the book. "No refunds or exchanges," he snapped, pointing to a sign on the counter.

"I don't want my money back," Ben said. "And I don't want anything else in the store. I just don't want the kit anymore."

"But I thought you wanted to be a great magician," Mr. Cream said.

That's odd, Ben thought. *I don't remember telling Mr. Cream that I wanted to be a great magician. How did he know that?*

The bell tinkled again, and a woman walked in the store. She smiled at them and then walked over to some glass display cases.

Ben turned back to Mr. Cream. "I do want to become a great magician," he said. "Just not like Dr. Presto."

"I see," Mr. Cream said. He picked up the magic kit. "Then I will certainly take it back."

Ben felt relieved. He turned to leave, then remembered something. "Uh, you're not going to sell this to anyone else, are you?" he asked.

"Of course not," Mr. Cream said. But as Ben walked away, he thought he heard the old man add, "Probably."

On the way out he passed the woman who had entered the store. She was staring at a necklace in the display case.

"May I look at this, please?" she asked Mr. Cream. "It looks like the perfect gift for my niece."

Ben stopped. He thought about warning the woman. He'd hate for anyone else to go through what he had just been through.

But Ben realized that was silly. Just because his magic kit had contained an evil spirit didn't mean that everything in the shop harbored some terrifying secret.

Did it?

THE END